CAROLINE D GRIMM

Town Farm Boy

This book is dedicated to my dear friend,
Michael J. Davis.
Your boundless enthusiasm for local history ensures stories will be uncovered and told for years to come. Thank you for all our dorky history conversations—I look forward to many more.

"What a man is made of is not the earth he
starts on, but the path he forges from it."

—Anonymous

Contents

Foreword

Dear Reader,

Welcome to the mythical town of Pondicherry, a place I have come to know and love through my research into the rich history of Bridgton, Maine. For years, I have chronicled the lives of its early inhabitants in my series, *Voices of Pondicherry*, keeping a tight rein on the historical facts, letters, and actual events that shaped their lives.

This book marks the beginning of a new journey. The *Tales of Pondicherry* series offers a different approach, one that embraces the freedom of fiction. While the world of Pondicherry is still firmly rooted in the historical flow of real events, I have given myself the creative liberty to weave imagined characters and their lives into the tapestry of that history. In some cases, real historical figures may be used in entirely fictional ways to explore the spirit of a time and place.

This new format allows for more dramatic storytelling and the freedom to delve into the untold possibilities that lie between the lines of historical records. But my commitment to honoring the past remains. At the end of each book in this series, you will find a **Fact vs. Fiction** section where I will clarify what is real and what has been invented.

I am delighted to invite you on this new adventure, and I look forward to exploring many more stories in the books to come.

Caroline D. Grimm

Prologue

Something you should know about me right off. My Ma is dead. Some say it's on account of me. I hope that ain't true because killing your own ma, especially when you're just being born, feels like the worst kind of wrong. Pastor Frye tells me it want my fault on account of the 'wages of sin being death.' I don't know about that. All I know is I ain't got a Ma. Nor a Pa neither. I don't reckon I killed him. I reckon he just up and disappeared because I killed my Ma. Seems a feller wouldn't take kindly to a baby for doing what I did. I don't know.

I guess folks don't know much what to do with a boy that hasn't got a Ma or a Pa. Pastor said some old soldier feller put some cash money aside for "the worthy and industrious poor" way back in the olden days. The old feller fought at Bunker Hill and I sure would like to hear him tell some stories about them days. Anyway, I'm not "worthy" on account of killing my Ma so I guess my lot is to be "industrious". Mr. Sanborn says that means I have to work extra hard doing chores and the like around the farm so's I earn my keep and I'm not a burden on the town.

Mr. Sanborn's an okay sort. His eyes would narrow to slits if he caught you leaning on your rake instead of putting some elbow grease into the business end of it. But he always makes sure there's extry maple syrup in the switchel when his missus hauls it out to the haying field for us workers. The last superintendent was more likely to add extry vinegar just to be a miserable cuss.

Me and Wesley and Ned share a room. Ned's all crippled up and he can't hardly get out of bed, but he's a good feller. He tells ripping good stories at night before we go to sleep. Me and Wesley have to help him do most things like changing his clothes and emptying his piss pot and bringing his breakfast tray.

Wesley is my friend. Everyone thinks he's an idiot but he ain't. When the others call him "dummy" or "simpleton," Wesley just blinks slow, like he's watching flies buzz. But me and him, we talk with our hands, slow and easy, and we get on just fine. He understands more than folks give him credit for.

Most of the rest are old folks. Or they have some kind of hitch in their giddyup or their brains ain't right or something. Two of the women folks get locked up all the time because they're not right in the head. Marylou usually takes care of them cause it ain't safe for anyone else to be near 'em. She always moves quiet around them, even when they's screeching. Marylou mostly does the washing and cleaning up which is a lot of work taking care of those old folks. Most of the folks here aren't "industrious" because of being old or broken so they must be the "worthy" poor that old Bunker Hill feller was talking about.

That's alright. Pastor says everyone gets different gifts. I keep waiting for mine.

Most days I go to school and I don't think much of that. My lot is to be industrious and school keeps me from doing that. Master Ingalls says I can be industrious at my schoolwork so I can be educated *and* industrious. Mostly, I'm just happy when he lets us out for recess.

Nobody from the farm goes to school with me except Nan. She's Mr. Sanborn's girl. She's little. She has nice clothes to wear. Not fancy nice, but clean and pressed nice. Her Ma makes sure of that. Me, I mostly am clean and patched and that's good enough for me. Mrs. Sanborn packs us both dinner to take to school. It's a bit of a walk so I carry Nan's dinner pail and books on account of her being littler than me. She likes school. I don't know why.

Mostly, I just like being outside. Outside a feller can hear what's going on in his own head. Inside is too busy and someone's always bossing me around. "Edwin, fetch this..." "Edwin, take this..." "Edwin, help me..." Being one of the industrious poor can sure be a lot of work.

But I can't complain much being as I'm a lucky feller having a roof over my head and food in my belly. Maybe that's more than I ought to have being who

I am and all. I don't know.

Part One

I

"A boy's worth is not to be measured by his name, but by the
work of his hands. Yet in this town, the only truth many will ever
see is the circumstance of his birth."
—From the desk of the Editor, Pondicherry Chronicle, 1885

Chapter 1

"Girl! I got some deliveries for you to make!"

"Yes, Papa." Hannah's shoulders hitched slightly as she spoke.

He thrust the basket into her arms. "Be quick about it!"

Hannah's mother, a quiet voice from the doorway, added, "Will you stop off at the apothecary and pick up my order while you're there, dear?"

"Of course, Mama." Hannah turned, already reaching for the familiar weight of her shawl.

Hannah drew her shawl tighter against the sharp October chill and set out on her errands. The sky overhead was a brilliant blue, a treasured "bluebird day" in Maine. Her first stop was Widow Kathro's house. As she dropped off the mended shoes, the old woman's lonely voice pleaded, "Oh, do stay, Hannah, for a cup of tea." Widow Kathro, solitary since her husband died, clung to any interaction.

"I'm sorry, ma'am," Hannah replied, already turning. Her feet were already moving toward the gate. "I can't stop today. My father needs these other deliveries made."

"That's alright, dear. You stop by when you can." Hannah gave a quick wave as she continued up Church Street. At the Riley's house, she handed off Mr. Riley's heavy work boots. Then, with the basket lighter, she headed for her last stop.

Knocking at the kitchen door, she was surprised when the head of the household, himself, answered. His presence filled the doorway, eclipsing the crisp morning light. A thick scent of bay rum and pipe tobacco preceded him.

"Hello, Sir," she began, her stomach giving a sudden, cold clench. "Here's your order from my father. He asked that I bring it by." She paused, the silence stretching awkwardly.

The man's eyes narrowed, impatience hardening his features. "What is it, girl? Spit it out. I'm a busy man."

"I'm sorry, Sir," she stammered, her voice barely a whisper. "My father asked that I pick up payment on your account while I'm here."

An angry scowl twisted his face, but then it smoothed, replaced by a chillingly pleasant expression. Sighing, he said, "Come in. Come in." She glanced around the kitchen, saw the man's half-eaten sandwich on the kitchen table. He turned, leading her deeper into the house, towards his study at the back. The hallway was dimmer than the kitchen, silent and still.

He motioned her in, and the heavy door clicked shut behind him. Hannah's stomach tightened. Leaning against the door, he said, "How old are you now, Hannah?"

"Sixteen, Sir," she answered politely, her voice thin. She felt suddenly small, exposed in the center of the room.

He smiled, a slow, appraising curve of his lips. "Have you got your sights set on some young man?" he asked.

"No, Sir," she said, a blush creeping up her face, fueled more by discomfort than shyness. Her skin felt hot, but her hands were icy cold.

"A fine-looking young woman like you? What is wrong with the young men of this town?"

Hannah hugged her basket tighter. "If you please, Sir, my mother is waiting for me to pick up her order at the apothecary, and I really must go."

He took a step closer. His shadow, thick and ominous, fell across the polished floorboards between them. "You can tell your mother you were detained. By me. She'll understand."

"Please, Sir, I need to leave. I need to go." Her voice trembled despite her efforts. The plea felt thin, lost in the heavy air of the room.

He moved closer still, his shadow falling over her. "You're not scared of me, girl, are you?" he asked, the question a taunt. He reached out, his fingers surprisingly cold as they took her chin. She flinched, instinctively recoiling.

She noticed bread crumbs on his cravat, an odd, small detail. His breath smelled of roast beef.

"You're as pretty as your mother was when she was your age," he murmured, his gaze sweeping over her. His hand slid from her chin to her shoulder, his grip firm, possessive. With his free hand, he pulled her toward him, crushing her against his coarse wool coat. She struggled, a small, trapped bird. She smelled the lanolin of his coat, felt the hard buttons pressing into her cheek. As she fought, his grip tightened, pressing her to him, then shoving her to the floor, the rough carpet scraping her knees. He slapped his hand over her mouth, silencing her panicked cry.

"Don't fight, pretty. Your mama didn't. She liked what I did. Just ask her."

He tore at her clothes, the sound of ripping fabric echoing in the small room. Her own frantic heartbeat seemed to thud in her ears, louder than the tearing cloth. His calloused hands pawed at her, mauling tender flesh. She froze, a rabbit terrified in the talons of a hawk, her body rigid and cold, her mind a blank, screaming canvas, but her body utterly still.

When he had done his worst, he hauled her roughly to her feet. Her dress was ripped at the shoulder, her underthings torn and ruined.

"That wasn't so bad, was it, kitten? And next time, you'll enjoy it more."

She sobbed, a ragged, choked sound, struggling to be released from his grip. "Let me go! Let me go!"

He grinned, a flash of white teeth. "I've no more use for you today." He leaned in, the scent of bay rum on his face, stale tobacco on his clothes. "If you breathe a word of this to anyone, I will make sure your father is ruined. Do you understand, girl? You'll all end up at the poor farm. You don't want that, do you, girl?"

She could only shake her head, tears blurring her vision. The image of her family in the dismal poor farm, cold and hungry, solidified in her mind, silencing the frantic clamor of her terror. He released her. She stumbled, pulling her shawl tightly around her, and ran.

She burst into her father's cooper shop, gasping, the familiar smells of wood shavings and leather suddenly alien. Her father looked up, irritation etched on his face. "Where you been, girl? I told you to hurry up!"

"I'm sorry, Papa," she choked out, her voice sounding dead, hollow, to her own ears. "I was...detained." The word tasted like ash.

"Gallivanting," he snorted, dismissing her. "Did you bring back payment like I told you to?"

She shook her head, unable to speak.

"Blast it, girl! You're no use to me at all!"

Her mother came in, about to ask about her apothecary order, but her words died in her throat. Taking one look at her daughter—the disarrayed shawl, the haunted eyes, the way she held herself—she motioned her into the house with a single, urgent glance.

Inside, her mother's hands were already on her shoulders, concern deeply furrowing her brow. "What happened?"

Hannah shook her head, unable to form words. She just wanted to disappear. To vanish like smoke.

"Tell me what happened."

Hannah started to sob, shaking her head back and forth, desperate. "Don't make me tell, Mama."

Her mother's face grew still, a mask of grim understanding. She knew then what had happened. And she knew who. It wasn't the first time. She gently dried Hannah's tears, her touch a stark contrast to the rough violation. Wrapping Hannah's own shawl more securely around her ruined clothing, she said, her voice low and steady, "Go. Go to your aunt. She'll know what to do. Don't say a word to anyone. I'll bring your things as soon as your father goes out. Town meeting is tomorrow. He'll be out for hours."

She opened the kitchen door, peering out to check for any curious eyes. "Go," she whispered, urgency in her tone. She paused, pulling Hannah close for a brief, fierce hug. "I love you, Hannah. I will see you as soon as I can."

July 7, 1867

In the upstairs chamber, Widow Foster leaned over the sweating form of the young woman. "You must tell," she insisted, her voice firm.

The woman writhed, her body trembling with contractions. "No!" she gasped, her voice raw with pain. "No!"

The servant woman gently mopped the young mother's sweaty brow, the cloth cool against her hot skin.

"They'll ask me, and I must tell them," the midwife pressed, relentless.

"No! No!" the woman exclaimed, her refusal weakening with each wave of agony.

Again, the demand was made. Again, she refused.

The contractions grew stronger, a relentless vise. The woman panted, a ragged moan escaping her lips.

"You must tell," the midwife pressed again, her voice unyielding. "Who is the father?" she demanded. "Tell me who the father of this babe is!"

With one final, exhausted push, her baby was thrust into an uncaring world, and the woman collapsed, spent, into the damp sheets.

"You have a son," she heard the midwife say, the words distant. *A son. Poor mite*, she thought, a fresh wave of grief and protectiveness washing over her.

"Who is the father of this boy? Name him now."

The woman turned her face to the wall, refusing to meet the midwife's gaze.

When the midwife was through with her work, the servant walked her to the door. "Mrs. Hutchins, if she says the name of the father, you must report it to the Overseers," the midwife warned, her tone sharp. The servant nodded, her expression grim. "I know my duty," she replied, her voice steady, hardened by years of quiet responsibility for her own family and now for the Sanborns, her old neighbors who had given her work when her own home was gone.

Later, as the woman lay with the babe at her breast, she stroked his tiny face with a tender touch, tracing the soft curve of his cheek. Looking up at Marylou Hutchins, she said, her voice clear despite her exhaustion, "His name is to be Edwin. Edwin Littlefield."

"He will not bear the father's name, then?" Marylou asked softly, her voice tinged with the familiar ache for her own sons, Abe Jr. and Robert, now so far away in Ohio, building lives she could only glimpse through letters.

"He will not," she responded, a fierce vehemence in her tone. "He must never know he has a son.”

"Will your son never know who his father is?”

"It's better that he doesn't.”

"Your secret is safe with me,” Marylou told her, laying a comforting hand on her arm. Her own husband, Abraham, lost to the war, had left her with so many secrets of her own heart. She understood the weight of buried truths.

Hannah's breath came in shallow gasps, each one a struggle that rattled her thin frame. Her eyes, sunken and clouded with fever, fixed on the tiny bundle Marylou held. Edwin. He was so small, so perfect in his innocence. Marylou, her own face grim, knelt beside the bed, one hand gently resting on Hannah's clammy forehead.

Hannah's hand, frail and cold, reached out, finding Marylou's rough palm. Her grip, surprisingly strong, tightened.

"Marylou,” she rasped, her voice barely a whisper, "Marylou, listen.”

Marylou bent closer, her heart aching. A mother's plea. She knew that ache, that fierce, primal need to protect and to be remembered. She thought of her own boys, long grown and far away, and the family life she once had, the one she still grieved. "I'm here, Hannah-girl. I'm listening.”

"My boy... my Edwin.” Hannah's eyes, brimming with an impossible love, welled with unshed tears. "Tell him, Marylou. When he's older. Tell him his Ma... his Ma loved him more than anything.” A tear traced a path down her temple. "Tell him... tell him it wasn't his fault. Not his. He's good. He's pure. He never... he never caused any of this.” Her voice faded, her grip weakening, but her gaze on the child, then on Marylou, held fierce. "Promise me, Marylou. Promise you'll tell him. He needs to know he was loved. Always.”

Marylou, tears stinging her own eyes, squeezed Hannah's hand. "I promise, Hannah. On my soul, I promise.”

"Thank you, Marylou. You've been a true friend to me.”

Hannah managed a faint, ghost of a smile, a flicker of peace on her pain-wracked face. Three days later, the infection ravaged her, draining her life until it claimed her, leaving behind only that promise and a babe alone and unprotected in the world.

Chapter 2

The Pondicherry night of early March of 1880 settled in with an unnatural stillness. A thin, cold mist clung to the lower reaches of Main Hill, muffling the usual evening creaks and whispers of the town. Coal oil lamps cast isolated pools of amber light from windows, and the occasional flickering gaslight on Main Street barely pierced the gloom, illuminating the skeletal branches of bare trees and the hushed facades of clapboard homes. Most respectable citizens were long abed, leaving the rugged streets to the occasional stray dog and the distant, rhythmic clatter of the late train from Portland. Pondicherry, for all its charm, knew the bite of fire. Years past, whole blocks had been swallowed, leaving scars that never quite faded from the town's collective memory.

Just after midnight, a solitary figure slipped from the shadows near the Pondicherry Railroad station. He was a nondescript man, dressed in plain business attire, carrying nothing but a small, heavy valise – the kind of man you'd see daily disembarking from a train in any city, and forget immediately. He moved with a practiced, unsettling purpose, blending into the deeper shadows of the side streets. He knew his target: the Littlefield cobbler shop, nestled neatly on the corner of Main Street and Fowler Street. It was an old, two-story building of dry, aged wood; the shop occupying the street level, the family living in the modest quarters above. A quick, practiced twist of a pick, a barely audible click, and a side door on Fowler Street opened into the shop's darkened interior.

Inside, the air was thick with the faint, familiar scents of leather and shoe polish. The man moved through the cluttered space with an almost surgical efficiency, guided by the dim glow of a small bullseye lantern. The heavy valise clunked softly as he set it down. A stopper was uncorked, and the distinct, acrid smell of kerosene began to bloom, quickly overwhelming the workshop's usual aroma. He moved swiftly, pouring a glistening trail of the accelerant from the door, across the worn floorboards, pooling it generously amongst the piles of leather scraps, bolts of fabric, and stacks of wooden lasts. This would be quick. This would be complete.

He struck a match.

The small flame sputtered, then caught, licking at the end of the kerosene trail. In an instant, with a furious whoosh, the liquid fire ignited, a low roar blossoming from the quiet room. The dry wood and flammable materials of the shop caught almost immediately, the heat blooming outwards with terrifying speed. Flames clawed their way up the walls, already licking at the wooden stairwell leading to the sleeping family above.

He slipped back into the shadows of Fowler Street as swiftly as he'd arrived. He didn't look back. His job was done. He moved with the same practiced, nondescript stride towards the station, where he'd secured passage on the early train. He was aboard and moving out of Pondicherry minutes later, a silent passenger among a few late-night railway men.

Behind him, on Main Hill, the Littlefield cobbler shop exploded in light and sound. The furious crackle of burning wood intensified, becoming a monstrous roar. Glass shattered from the street-level windows, spraying shards onto Main Street, followed by billows of thick, choking smoke that poured from the upstairs windows, blackening the night.

The first scream tore through the pre-dawn stillness – a woman's terrified shriek. Then another, a man's bellow. Soon, the desperate, frantic clang of the church bell began, tearing at the fabric of the night, rousing the entire town from its slumber. Sleepy, disoriented figures stumbled from their homes, drawn by the terrifying orange glow now painting the sky above Main Hill.

Neighbors rushed into the street, forming desperate, disorganized bucket lines, their faces illuminated by the inferno, contorted with horror. A hand-pumper engine, drawn by a single horse, clattered onto Main Street, its volunteer crew already straining to get water. They quickly ran their hoses to

Crotched Pond, a stone's throw from the shop, hoping the abundant water would be enough to quell the raging inferno. But the old wooden building on the corner was a tinderbox, consumed with impossible speed. The heat radiating onto Main Street was intense, driving them back. Through the smoke and fire, the horrifying realization spread – the Littlefields were inside. Trapped.

The heat was so immense that it wasn't long before sparks, like malevolent embers, leaped across the narrow alleyway and caught the dry shingles of Dr. Wilson's residence, located just behind the Littlefield's on Fowler Street. Soon, that building too began to glow with an ominous, secondary orange, adding to the growing conflagration. The screams faded into the roar of the fire, replaced by the shouts of men trying futilely to contain the blaze, and the growing sobs of women watching the tragedy unfold. The fear of widespread property loss, a specter from Pondicherry's past, hung heavy in the smoke-filled air.

Dawn broke over a scene of utter devastation. Where the Littlefield cobbler shop and home had stood on the corner of Main Street and Fowler Street, only a smoking, skeletal ruin remained. Directly behind it, on Fowler Street, Dr. Wilson's residence was also a charred shell, its roof collapsed, a testament to the fire's hungry spread. The air hung thick with the acrid smell of ash, wet char, and a faint, unsettling chemical scent that some of the volunteer firemen, wiping soot from their brows, exchanged uneasy glances about.

Among the stunned onlookers, her shawl clutched tightly around her, stood Rebecca Lewis. Her face was ashen, mirroring the gray dawn. Her eyes, usually calm and kind, were wide with a horrifying mix of grief and dawning terror. Her fingers, bone-white, dug into the woolen fabric of her shawl. She saw the smoking ruins of her sister's home, the place where she'd known a lifetime of shared laughter and quiet comfort. The image of her sister, warm and vibrant, flashed before her, now reduced to ash. Grief tore at her, sharp and unbearable, for her sister, the last of her family but one.

But beneath the sorrow, a chilling thought began to solidify, turning her stomach to ice. The fire's unnatural speed, its devouring completeness—this was no accident. It felt too deliberate. Her gaze, sharpened by a terrifying realization, swept across the smoldering landscape, searching for an answer she dared not speak. The faint, acrid scent of kerosene, clinging stubbornly to the cool morning air, whispered of something more than tragedy, and of danger. A shiver, not of cold, but of pure dread, traced its way down her spine. Rebecca's thoughts immediately turned to the fragile life she knew was safe, for now. He was nowhere near the blaze, unaware of the fresh hell that had just befallen his already precarious life. And he had to remain unaware. She would draw no attention to him, utter no word that might link him to this catastrophe, or to the dangerous undercurrents she now felt rippling beneath the town's surface. She knew, with chilling certainty, that she had to keep him safe, whatever the cost, from the unknown shadows that had just consumed his family.

Pondicherry Town Farm

The familiar clatter of the stove grate signaled that Marylou was already up, a phantom in the predawn gloom, her movements sharp and efficient. Edwin swung his feet onto the cold floor, the worn planks creaking beneath his weight. He hastily pulled on his patched overalls. As he tugged his work shirt over his head, Wesley, in the cot beside him, opened one eye and grinned, a sly, sleepy smile.

"Sure, it's alright for you to lay abed," Edwin muttered, good-naturedly. Wesley merely nodded, his grin widening. "Lucky old boy, you are."

Across the small room, Ned Lakin didn't stir, a lump under his thin blanket. Like Edwin, Ned was an orphan, though his path to the Town Farm had been crueler. His mother had died young, and his father, a timberman, had remarried. Then, a few years back, a logging accident had claimed his father's life and left Ned with a compound fracture in his leg, untreated and crooked. His stepmother, cold and quick to shed burdens, had simply sent him to Superintendent Sanborn. Now, largely confined to his bed, Ned's world was the room under the eaves and the pages of whatever books Mr. Sanborn could find. He spent his days devouring tales of high seas and daring heroes, and his nights recounting them to Edwin and Wesley. *Up late again reading,* Edwin thought, a familiar sigh catching in his throat. Matron would have it out for him when she found out how many candles he'd burned through this time. "Economy!" she'd preach, her voice like a rusty hinge.

Edwin tied on his work boots, the laces stiff and familiar, and clumped down the narrow stairs to the second floor.

"Edwin!" Matron's voice, sharp and immediate, cut through the quiet. "Easy on those stairs! You'll wake the dead!"

"Sorry, Ma'am," he replied, chastened, his footsteps instantly softened.

More quietly, he descended the last flight of stairs and pushed into the still-chilly kitchen. The air smelled faintly of woodsmoke and yesterday's cooking.

"Morning, Edwin," Marylou said, her voice a low rumble, her gaze fond. At fifty-one, with her husband Abraham lost to the war years ago and her sons Abe Jr. and Robert out in Ohio building their own lives, she found a quiet purpose in the rhythms of the Town Farm, a familiar routine that dulled the edges of her own loneliness.

"Mornin', Ma'am." He took the bucket of kitchen scraps she handed him, the weight familiar in his grasp. He headed out the kitchen door, leaping off the steps with a youthful burst of energy. The bucket sloshed, spilling a trail of slop. Marylou knocked once on the windowpane, a soft, knowing rap. He dipped his head by way of apology, a sheepish grin touching his lips.

On the way to the pigpen, he ducked into the outhouse to relieve himself, brushing away the sticky spiderwebs from the doorway. He buttoned up his fly, the coarse fabric stiff against his fingers, and picked up the bucket. The pigs, hidden from view but sensing his approach, set to squealing with eager anticipation as soon as they heard the outhouse door slam shut. Edwin quickened his pace in their direction. He dumped the slops into the trough, the sound a wet thud, and paused for a moment to enjoy the pure, unadulterated enthusiasm of the pigs digging into the scraps. Their snorts and grunts were a strange kind of music.

Next, he headed to the chicken coop. He unlatched the door and shooed the hens off their nests, their indignant squawks echoing in the dim light. The rooster, a puffed-up bundle of feathers, gave him a baleful look, his comb a fiery red. Edwin stomped his foot, and the rooster, offended but compliant, strutted out into the barnyard. From a hook just inside the coop door, Edwin lifted the woven egg basket. Edwin carefully gathered the eggs, near a dozen today, still warm from the hens. Marylou would be pleased with that. When the hens produced well, there was a better chance of a cake, maybe even an apple spice cake made from last year's hoarded applesauce. *A feller can dream,* he thought, a small, hopeful smile playing on his lips.

He carted the eggs back to the kitchen door, carefully handing the over-flowing basket to Marylou. From the barn, Bessie lowed, a deep, resonant call.

"Be right there," he muttered to himself, not to Marylou. "I've only got two hands and two feet."

Pulling open the big barn door took all his thirteen-year-old might. He was hit by a rush of smells: the sweet, dusty scent of hay from the loft, that warm, earthy animal smell, and the pungent tang of manure. *I'll get to that later,* he thought, wrinkling his nose. He listened to the cow shifting restlessly in her stall. The horses snorted and whickered to him, their breath steaming in the cool air. The oxen stood placid and calm in their pens, patiently awaiting their morning feed.

He grabbed the milking stool and bucket, the cold metal biting at his fingers, and let himself into Bessie's stall. "Easy, girl," he murmured, stroking her broad side as he filled her manger with fresh hay. He sat down on the stool, the wood smooth from years of use. With sure, practiced hands, he milked her, the rhythmic hiss of warm milk hitting the bucket with a comforting sound. Sometimes, as he sat with his head resting on the cow's warm side, surrounded by the peaceful sounds of the barn, he'd imagine this was his own farm, his barn, his animals. And inside, his family. His own Ma and Pa...he stopped himself, gave his head a shake. That was too much to dream of for someone like him. Bessie shifted, annoyed with the delay. "Easy, girl," he crooned. He stripped each teat carefully, coaxing the last drops. "There you go," he said soothingly. Her milk would dry up soon. Mr. Johnson's bull would be needed for breeding before long.

Carrying the milk bucket carefully, its contents sloshing gently, he walked back to the kitchen door. He handed it to Marylou, who took it with a nod and placed it on the counter in the pantry.

"Wash up, now," she said, her voice soft but firm, nodding towards the wash basin outside the door. Her voice, though gentle, carried the quiet authority of years spent managing a household, a skill she'd cultivated first in her own home with Abraham and her boys, and now here, as a servant, though the Sanborns treated her more like family.

Expecting the slap of cold water, he braced himself. But as he plunged his hands in, he was surprised to find a hint of warmth. He glanced toward the kitchen window, a small smile spreading across his wet face. Marylou gave him a quick, knowing wink. She was like that. Now and then, she'd surprise him with a little treat, a small, unexpected kindness that made the hard edges of his life a little softer. She was a woman of many useful skills—cooking, cleaning, preserving food, even treating minor ailments—but it was these quiet acts of compassion that truly set her apart.

Just then, the familiar rumble of wheels on the rutted lane announced a visitor. Marylou glanced out the window, a subtle shift in her expression. "It's Mrs. Lewis," she murmured, a note of quiet anticipation in her voice. She valued Mrs. Lewis's visits, not just for the break in routine, but for the chance to share a moment of quiet understanding with another woman of conscience in the community.

Edwin knew Mrs. Lewis. He had known Mrs. Lewis his whole life. She was a constant, kind presence, one of the few who consistently visited the Farm. She was a pillar of the Pondicherry Village Church, known for her tireless benevolence. She arrived often, with baskets of mended clothes from the Ladies' Aid Society, or sometimes a pie still warm from her oven, her official reason always to "check on the welfare of the town's charges."

As Mrs. Lewis stepped from her buggy, her posture erect and her smile warm, she exchanged greetings with Edwin. "Good morning, Edwin," she called, her voice clear and kind. "A fine start to the day, it seems."

"Morning, Ma'am," Edwin replied, self-conscious but grateful for the politeness.

She then entered the kitchen, where Marylou had already set out a small tea tray. Mrs. Lewis and Marylou settled at the scrubbed pine table. Their conversation was soft, polite, mostly about church doings and the town's quiet affairs, but Edwin, ever observant, noticed the way their heads would often lean in, their voices dropping to hushed tones. Sometimes, their eyes would meet across the room, a flicker of something he couldn't decipher passing between them, a shared understanding he knew nothing about. He just knew they were talking about the kind of quiet, important things women talked about, the things his own ma would've talked about with her friends, if he'd ever had a ma who talked to friends.

After some time, Mrs. Lewis prepared to leave, offering a final, soft smile and a general farewell before her buggy crunched back down the drive.

Edwin finished washing his hands, a new lightness in his step from the break in routine. Mrs. Lewis was like that. Always a quiet moment, a subtle change to the Farm's usual drone. He wondered what conversations she and Marylou had, what quiet stories they exchanged when they leaned in close like that. Were they like the adventures Ned spun from his books—tales of faraway places and brave deeds—or just the everyday talk of women, the kind he still didn't quite understand?

After Mrs. Lewis had left, leaving a quiet echo in the kitchen, Edwin finished his chores. He knew what came next, breakfast and a hard day's work. July meant haying, a brutal race against the weather to secure enough winter feed for the animals. Every available hand at the Town Farm, along with neighbors, would be out in the fields from sunup to sundown. It was a time of intense, interdependent labor, where success meant survival and failure could mean starvation.

As Edwin approached the barn, Mr. Sanborn, the Superintendent, stood near a cart, supervising Silas as he finished hitching a sturdy draft horse. Wesley, his head tilted at a curious angle, was nearby, attempting to untangle a piece of rope, more hindrance than help. Other men, mostly neighbors who had come to lend their skill and brawn for this essential harvest, milled about, gathering scythes and rakes. Some knelt, meticulously sharpening their blades, drawing out the thin, razor edge necessary for a day's cutting.

Leander Frost, his usually tidy hair already ruffled by the early breeze, was among them, his brow furrowed in concentration as he tested the sharpness of his own scythe. Mr. Sanborn, a man of few words but firm commands, turned to face them all.

"Alright, boys! Sun's climbing. We've got a good window for it today," he announced, his voice carrying clearly. "Silas, you and this first wagon take the north section. Edwin, you're with Cyrus on the west field. We'll start cutting there and let it cure. The rest of you, follow along, keep the rows clean." He paused, glancing briefly at Wesley. "Wesley, you can stay near the water buckets."

Edwin nodded, already moving toward the stack of scythes. As he grabbed his, he heard it: a booming laugh from near the west field's edge, followed by a clear, strong voice ringing out across the fields, several voices joining him, some humming, some singing the words with gusto: "Blessed assurance, Jesus is mine! O what a foretaste of glory divine! Heir of salvation, purchase of God, Born of His Spirit, washed in His blood."

It was Cyrus Cross, a spare man, thin and spry, a man known for his poetry and music. He was an exceptionally competent farmer, his skill with a scythe almost an art form. His bald head gleaming in the sun. But every few strokes, he'd pause, his blue eyes twinkling as he'd offer a quick, rhyming couplet about the dusty joy of the harvest. "Steady now, young Edwin!" he called out, his scythe rising and falling with a flourish that seemed more performative than practical. "For every blade of grass you fell, a poem of summer's bounty I shall tell!" He winked. Edwin couldn't help but smile. Cyrus, with his bright eyes and quick wit, made even the hardest work feel lighter.

The hours blurred into a haze of sweat and sun. The air grew thick with the scent of cut grass, the dry hay piling into fragrant mounds behind them. The rhythmic swish-swish of scythes filled the field, a steady song of labor. Edwin found himself working alongside Leander Frost for a stretch, their scythes rising and falling in unison. Leander, usually busy with his own farm, matched Edwin's steady pace, his earlier casual observations replaced by a quiet, focused determination. Leander was seeing, firsthand, the unyielding effort Edwin put into every swing, the sheer grit that defined the boy's every task.

Edwin's shoulders ached, and dust clung to his throat, but the camaraderie of the other men and Cyrus's endless stream of jingles kept him going. They'd cut the hay today, leave it to dry in the sun, and tomorrow or the next, they'd haul it to the barn.

Just before noon, a welcome sight appeared at the edge of the field: Marylou, her sturdy frame silhouetted against the bright sun, carrying a large pail and a stack of tin cups. "Switchel!" a cry went up from the men. She poured Edwin a cup. He gulped it down, the tangy, sweet, and spicy liquid cutting through the dust and heat, strangely refreshing despite its sharp, vinegary kick. "Thank you, Marylou," he rasped, feeling a burst of renewed energy.

Their work done, the men made their way towards Foster Pond, the promise of its cool depths a powerful lure. The laughter started low, a rumble of anticipation, then erupted into shouts as they reached the water's edge. Without ceremony, they stripped down to their drawers, their aching bodies eager for relief. Edwin plunged in, the shock of the cold water stealing his breath for a moment before the delicious chill spread through his sun-baked skin. Splashing and ducking, hooting and hollering, they cleansed away the dust and sweat of the fields, the day's fatigue momentarily forgotten in the pure joy of the cool water. Even Amos Sanborn, normally so composed, let out a boyish whoop as he dove under, surfacing with a grin.

That evening, around the scrubbed pine table, the Town Farm kitchen was filled with the sounds of hardworking men laughing and joking at the end of a satisfying day in the fields. The air, though thick with the scent of woodsmoke and the lingering humidity of the day, offered a respite from the blazing sun. Marylou's simple beef stew, thick with potatoes and carrots, was passed around, its aroma a powerful draw. Cyrus, soon on his second helping, raised his spoon with a theatrical flourish. "Ah, Marylou!" he boomed, his voice echoing in the cozy space. "This stew! A symphony of sustenance! A veritable ode to honest labor! Never have simple spuds and beef sung so gloriously to the soul of a hungry man!" He smacked his lips with exaggerated pleasure. "One could work twice as hard for such a reward, eh, lads?" He caught Edwin's eye, a shared understanding passing between them.

◆

The thin walls under the eaves did little to keep out the heat of the long summer day. It didn't just linger; it pressed in from every surface, an oppressive blanket woven from the day's relentless sun. Even now, hours after dusk, the air held a close, breathless warmth, slow to yield. Edwin lay on his cot, staring up at the shadowy rafters. Beside him, Wesley was already a lump under his blanket, soft snores filling the silence. Across the small room, Ned shifted, his own cot springs groaning in protest. Unable to get up much, Ned spent most of his days lost in the pages of books Marylou or Mr. Sanborn managed to acquire, their stories vivid in his mind.

"You awake, Edwin?" Ned whispered, his voice a low rustle in the dark.

"Sure."

A moment of quiet passed, broken only by Wesley's steady breathing and the distant chirp of crickets.

"Too tired for a story, Edwin?" Ned asked, his voice suddenly alight with a different kind of energy. "I've got a good adventure story tonight."

Edwin shifted and turned towards Ned's cot. "Never too tired for a story, Ned."

"Today while you were all out in the fields, I read a good one." Ned's voice rose in excitement. "It's about a man named Captain Ahab. From that book Mr. Sanborn lent me. He chased a white whale across the whole ocean, just for spite."

"A whale?" Edwin mumbled, a sliver of curiosity cutting through his weariness.

"A monstrous one! White as snow, with a jaw like a trap. Captain Ahab lost his leg to it, see, and swore he'd get his revenge. They sailed for months, through storms and calm, looking for this one whale." Ned's voice grew animated, painting vivid pictures in the dark room. He described the vastness of the ocean, the dangers, the single-minded obsession.

Edwin listened, half-dreaming, the rhythmic rise and fall of Ned's voice blending with Wesley's snores and the crickets outside. He'd never seen the ocean, only heard distant tales. But for a few moments, Ned's words took him far beyond the confines of the Town Farm, into a world of obsession and vast, wild spaces.

When Ned finally trailed off, having finished the latest installment of his retelling, a deeper quiet descended upon the small room. Edwin listened to the distant chorus of bull frogs from the pond, and to Wesley's rhythmic snores. Another day was done. Another night under the sheltering roof of the Town Farm.

Chapter 3

The summer sun poured through the open window, painting warm stripes across the worn wooden floorboards of the Small family's parlor. Dust motes danced in the golden light, a silent ballet that only a child truly noticed. Four-year-old Jane, called Jenny, her dark curls catching the light like a halo, hummed a tuneless, happy song as she meticulously arranged a tiny patchwork quilt over her most treasured possession: a homemade rag doll with button eyes and yarn hair, whom she called Jenny Wren.

"There, there, my dear," Jenny cooed, patting the doll's head. "Nice and cozy. No bad dreams today." She tucked the doll in securely, then leaned back on her heels, a satisfied smile spreading across her face.

From his armchair by the hearth, where a cool breeze drifted in despite the warmth of the day, Mr. Small watched his daughter. His pipe lay unlit on a small table beside him, forgotten in the quiet joy of the moment. He had a strong, kind face, softened by the lines around his eyes that crinkled when he smiled, which was often when he looked at Jenny.

"And what grand adventures are you two planning today, my little wren?" he asked, his voice a low, gentle rumble. A chuckle began deep in his chest before he even finished the question.

Jenny giggled, a sound like tiny bells. "Oh, Daddy! Jenny Wren is going to have a tea party! And then we're going to visit the fairies in the woods at the edge of the field!" She pointed vaguely toward the window, her eyes wide with the conviction only a child can possess.

Mr. Small chuckled, a warm sound that filled the room. "To the fairy woods, you say? Well, make sure you're very polite, and perhaps they'll show you where they hide their wishing dust."

Jenny's eyes widened further, full of wonder and delight at his playful suggestion. "Wishing dust, Daddy! Yes! A whole pocketful!" She scrambled to her feet, her bare feet padding softly on the rug, and began to dance around the room, twirling her doll, a small, bright, happy bird in her father's loving gaze. The sunshine seemed to follow her, illuminating every joyful leap and spin. In that moment, the world was perfect, held safe and warm within the walls of their little home, under the watchful, adoring eyes of her daddy.

Later that August afternoon, after Jenny had finally succumbed to a nap, her small form curled around her doll, Thomas Small unfolded the latest edition of the *Pondicherry Chronicle.* The headlines screamed of battles, of casualties, of the endless grind of war. But his eye drifted to a smaller, boxed advertisement towards the bottom of the page:

"MEN WANTED FOR THE UNION CAUSE! GENEROUS BOUNTIES OFFERED! $800 FOR VOLUNTEERS! PROTECT YOUR HOMES! SERVE YOUR COUNTRY!"

He chewed on the stem of his unlit pipe, his gaze flicking from the bold print to the sleeping child, then to the worn elbows of his own jacket. Times had been lean. The farm wasn't producing what it used to, and the cost of everything seemed to creep higher by the week. He'd resisted the calls to arms for years, couldn't bear the thought of leaving Jane, of missing a moment of her growing up. The thought of her small hand in his, her bright laughter echoing in the parlor, had always been enough to anchor him.

His wife, Sarah, entered the room, her face etched with a familiar weariness. She saw the newspaper in his hand, saw where his gaze lingered.

"Thomas," she began, her voice soft but firm, "the boys down the road, the Millers... their eldest just signed up. Two hundred dollars of their bounty went straight to fixing that leaky roof. Think of what eight hundred could do for us. For Jane."

He flinched at the mention of their daughter, the very reason he had stayed, now used as the reason he should go. He pictured Jenny, dancing with her doll, chasing imaginary fairies. The bounty was a fortune. Enough to secure them for years, enough to fix the drafty barn, maybe even buy that extra cow. The war, they said, couldn't last much longer. Surely he'd be home before the bitter cold set in. He looked at the quiet parlor, then out to the tired fields. The duty, the money, the subtle pressure in Sarah's eyes... and the image of his little girl, needing a better future.

He sighed, a heavy sound that stirred the quiet air. The pipe remained unlit.

The latch on the front gate clicked, a sound that had echoed in Jane's dreams for months. "Daddy's home!" she squealed, dropping Jenny Wren the doll mid-tea party and scrambling to the door, her heart hammering against her ribs like a trapped bird. She flung it open, her eyes bright with anticipation.

But as she drew closer, a wave of confusion washed over her, quickly followed by a sharp sting of fear. One side of his face was a landscape of puckered, angry scars, pulling his mouth into a grim, unfamiliar line. One eye looked clouded and distant, the other held a flicker of something she didn't recognize—a weariness that seemed to weigh him down more than his crutch. The familiar scent of him—pipe tobacco and clean linen—was gone, replaced by something metallic and sharp, like old blood.

He didn't scoop her up in a joyous hug. He didn't ruffle her hair and call her his "little wren." He just stood there, his good eye fixed on her with an expression she couldn't decipher. His arms hung stiffly at his sides, as if weighted.

"Jane," he said, his voice raspy, a mere shadow of the warm, booming sound she remembered telling her stories. He didn't reach for her.

She stopped a few feet away, her outstretched arms falling to her sides. "Daddy?" she whispered, her bright excitement faltering. This man looked like her daddy, but something was terribly wrong.

He shifted his weight on the crutch, a sigh escaping his lips that sounded more like a groan. He saw the horror bloom in her wide, innocent eyes, the confusion deepening her brow. He saw the small, unsure step she took back, and the hope drain from her face. His hand, which had trembled as he gestured to his ruined face, dropped to his side, heavy and useless.

"Yes, Jenny," he managed, his voice barely a whisper, thick with an anguish that had nothing to do with his physical wounds. "It's me. The war... it changes things."

She stared at the scars, her innocent mind struggling to reconcile this frightening image with the kind, smiling face she held so dearly in her memory. But it wasn't just his face. His shoulders, once broad and strong when he lifted her high in the air, now seemed slumped and defeated. His eyes, once full of laughter when he played with her, now held a deep, unreadable sadness.

He didn't ask about her tea party, or if she'd seen the fairies. He didn't ask about Jenny Wren the doll. He simply stood there, a stranger in the familiar shape of her beloved father, the sunshine doing little to dispel the heavy shadow that seemed to cling to him. The air, once filled with the promise of "Daddy's coming home," now felt cold and still, carrying a silent message: the daddy she had longed for was home, but he wasn't the same. Not at all.

The barn was usually a place of comforting smells: hay, dry earth, and the warm, sleepy scent of the cow. Six-year-old Jane had wandered in, her dolly Jenny Wren clutched tight. Her official reason was a lost ribbon, but more so seeking a quiet corner away from the tense silence that had settled over the house since Daddy came home. But deeper down, a child's unwavering hope propelled her, always looking for him, for the Daddy she remembered—the one who called her Jenny Wren and believed in fairies and wishing dust. Her mother had gone to town, leaving a palpable, anxious stillness in her wake.

A sliver of light, dust-filled and lazy, cut across the main beam near the loft ladder. Jane's gaze drifted upwards, idly following the path of the sunlight.

And then she saw it.

It wasn't immediately clear. Just a dark shape hanging oddly from the beam, swaying ever so slightly. Her child's mind, still steeped in the magic of fairies and tea parties, struggled to make sense of the strange, unmoving form.

"Daddy?" she whispered, a thin, reedy sound swallowed by the vast, silent barn. Her heart, which had been so quick and playful, now felt like a cold stone in her chest.

She took a step closer, then another, her bare feet silent on the packed earth floor. The sunlight shifted, catching on something familiar: the worn fabric of his trousers, the outline of his heavy boots. And then, as her eyes adjusted, as her innocent brain desperately tried to connect the familiar shape with this impossible sight, the reality slammed into her. The smell hit her then—something sharp and metallic, like the coppers her daddy used to give her at the store for sweets, but mixed with something else, something cloying and sickly sweet.

It was Daddy. But he wasn't standing. He was hanging. From the beam.

A high, thin cry caught in her throat, a sound she didn't know she could make. Her world, already shadowed by his return, now exploded into a million shards of terrifying, incomprehensible darkness. The safe, sun-drenched parlor, the comforting rumble of his laughter, the promise of wishing dust – all of it was instantly, violently, irrevocably gone.

Her fingers, suddenly slack and numb, unclenched. Jenny Wren, the doll, tumbled silently to the dusty floor, landing on her back. Her little button eyes, fixed and unblinking, stared blankly up at the swaying figure above, silent, unseeing witnesses to the unspeakable. Jane stood rooted to the spot, her breath frozen in her lungs, her wide, horrified eyes fixed on the man who was and was not her father. The barn, once a haven of simple, earthy smells, now reeked of something else, something cold and final. The sound she made was not a scream, but a choked, silent splintering. The silence of the barn swallowed her, and in that silence, a child's mind retreated.

The air in the receiving room of the Augusta Insane Hospital was thick with the scent of carbolic soap and damp wool, a stark contrast to the fresh country air Jane remembered. Dr. Alistair Baxter scribbled notes on his pad, barely glancing up as Nurse Agnes Miller presented the new admission.

"Patient Jane Small, admitted this afternoon, Doctor," Nurse Miller stated, her voice brisk but with a hint of fatigue. "Sent from Dr. Farnsworth in Pondicherry."

Dr. Baxter made a small grunt of acknowledgment. "Details, Nurse."

Nurse Miller consulted a clipboard. "Born 1861, making her twelve years of age. Father, a Mr. Thomas Small, was a Civil War veteran. Sustained severe physical injuries, returned... much changed. Suffered from 'soldier's heart,' according to Dr. Farnsworth. Committed suicide by hanging in the family barn when the patient was six years old. The patient... discovered the body."

Dr. Baxter's pen paused. "Ah. A profound shock, then."

"Indeed, Doctor. Dr. Farnsworth reports her mother lost herself in grief immediately after her husband's death. Neglected the child, immersed herself in society. Remarried a couple of years ago to a Mr. Harrison, who, by all accounts, is entirely indifferent to the girl. He is said to call her 'the child' rather than by her name." Nurse Miller glanced towards the small, huddled figure on a bench in the corner.

Jane sat motionless, her knees drawn up to her chest, her arms wrapped tightly around a worn rag doll with button eyes and yarn hair. Her lips moved silently, forming words that no one else could hear.

"Dr. Farnsworth reports she never truly recovered," Nurse Miller continued, her voice softening slightly as she looked at Jane. "He claims she became 'queer in the head' almost immediately. Always quiet, withdrawn. Rarely spoke, and when she did, it was often in a small, childlike voice. And constantly with that doll."

Dr. Baxter followed her gaze. "The doll. What does she call it?"

"Jenny Wren, Doctor. And the peculiar thing is, sometimes she calls herself Jenny Wren too. She seems to believe she is that age, six years old, just before... the incident. She's remarkably sensitive to loud noises or sudden movements, becomes quite agitated. And Dr. Farnsworth mentioned her often trying to wander off, talking about 'visiting the fairies in the woods.' Apparently, that was something her father indulged before he... well."

The doctor nodded slowly, looking at Jane with a detached clinical assess-ment. "Melancholy, certainly. Extreme withdrawal, regression, anhedonia.

It would seem the trauma has fractured her deeply." He scribbled rapidly. "We'll begin with sedatives, a nourishing diet, and observation. Nurse, ensure she is kept in a quiet ward. We shall see if time, and proper care, can coax Miss Small back to us."

Nurse Miller murmured an affirmation, but as she looked at the child rocking gently on the bench, clutching her doll, she couldn't shake the feeling that Jane Small might never truly return. Only Jenny Wren remained.

The air in Amos Sanborn's cramped office at the Town Farm smelled perpetually of boiled cabbage and unwashed wool. Outside the single grimy window, the late autumn wind whipped across the barren fields, rattling the loose panes. Sanborn, a barrel-chested man with a perpetually stern jaw, sat opposite Josiah Croft, one of the town's Overseers of the Poor. Croft, a man whose tailored suit seemed ill-suited to the grim surroundings, cleared his throat, a faint distaste on his face.

"So, Sanborn, you've received the transfer papers for the Small girl?" Croft asked, gesturing vaguely towards a stack of documents on the corner of Sanborn's cluttered desk. "Jane Small. Coming over from the Augusta hospital. They sent the particulars."

Sanborn sighed, pulling a yellowed document closer. "Yes, Croft. Got 'em this morning. Nineteen years she is, according to this. Nineteen years old, and they've had her at the hospital since she was twelve." He rubbed a hand over his tired face. "That's a long time for a soul to be away from proper family."

Croft nodded, a flicker of strained regret in his gaze. "Indeed, Amos. The town simply can't bear the expense any longer. The hospital bills for her care alone could fund a new schoolhouse. Dr. Baxter at the asylum assures us she's 'subdued' now, unlikely to require the specialized attention of a mental institution. She doesn't present a danger, merely... a considerable cost to the public purse." He paused, adjusting his spectacles. "Her condition stems from the family tragedy I know we all remember, Amos. Her father, Thomas

Small, the veteran who lived just down the road here from the farm, took his own life when Jane was but six. She discovered him."

Sanborn's gaze softened, a deep furrow appearing between his brows. "Poor child. Thomas. I remember him well. Good man, before the war took his spirit. Soldier's heart. Saw plenty of good men broken by that war. And for a little one to witness such a thing..." He shook his head slowly. "All those years, and she's still grieving, I suppose."

"Her mother, Sarah, as you know, lost herself in grief immediately after the husband's death," Croft continued. "Neglected the girl, apparently. Remarried a Mr. Harrison from over Buxton way, a man quite indifferent to the child, by all accounts. So, Jane was sent directly to Augusta shortly after the remarriage. Been there ever since."

"And her condition now?" Sanborn pressed, his voice quiet, almost compassionate. "What's this 'melancholy' they scribble about? And the 'regression'?"

"She's withdrawn, mostly," Croft explained. "Quiet. Dr. Baxter noted she rarely speaks, and when she does, it's often in a small, childlike voice. And she carries a doll, apparently. Calls it 'Jenny Wren,' and sometimes calls herself that too, believing she's still that six-year-old. She tries to wander off occasionally, looking for some 'fairy woods,' as her father once indulged. But they assure us she's easily redirected now. Mellower. Subdued."

Sanborn closed his eyes for a moment, picturing the girl who was coming. He wasn't a doctor, but he'd seen enough broken people in his life. When he opened them, his expression was weary, but resolute. "Mellower. Yes. Well, we'll do our best for her here. It won't be like the hospital, but she'll have a roof over her head, warm food, and a place to be. We'll make sure she's looked after, Josiah. There's only work and practical comfort here, but sometimes that's all a body can give." He picked up his pipe, carefully packing it with tobacco. The simple, ritualistic act was a comfort, a small defiance against the grim duty ahead.

Croft merely nodded, rising to his feet, a flicker of relief evident in his posture. His duty was done, the town's burden lightened. And Sanborn, for his part, braced himself for the quiet, broken soul about to enter his care.

Chapter 4

Cedar Mountain, Culpepper, Virginia

The August air in the Virginia cornfield was a humid, suffocating blanket, thick with the smell of trampled stalks, gunpowder, and something else—something metallic and sweet that made Silas Andrews's stomach churn. He gripped his musket, the wood slick with sweat, his heart hammering against his ribs like a panicked drum. He'd joined the 10th Maine in the spring of '62, alongside a score of other Pondicherry lads, including Billy Miller, the son of a local farmer, and Arthur Jordan, known back home for his strong arm at the forge, a skill that made him valuable even here in this hellscape, shoeing the officers' horses. Silas and Arthur, near the same age, had shared stories of home and horses during the long marches, their Maine roots a silent bond in this distant, hostile land. The vague notions of duty and adventure Silas had once held had evaporated somewhere between the unending marches and the first distant crackle of rifle fire.

Now, the crackle was a roar. The cornstalks around him exploded in splintered shards, ripped apart by what sounded like angry hornets. He ducked, pushing his face into the dirt, feeling the vibrations of unseen artillery shells thudding into the earth nearby. A yell, high-pitched and choked, tore through the din just to his left. He risked a glance. Billy Miller, whose laughter had filled the Pondicherry general store just months ago, lay crumpled amongst the green leaves, a dark stain spreading rapidly across his chest. His eyes, wide and unseeing, stared up at the relentless summer sky. A fly, insolent and fat, landed on Billy's open eye.

"Forward! For God's sake, forward!" A sergeant, his face black with powder, screamed, waving his sword.

Silas pushed himself up, his knee protesting as a sharp pain shot through it—not a hit, just the constant ache of the march. He stumbled forward, reloading his musket with fumbling hands, the rhythmic chant of "Load, ram, fire!" lost in the sheer, overwhelming chaos. Men fell beside him, some with a gurgle, others with a silent slump, disappearing into the tall corn as if swallowed by the earth itself. The air shrieked with minie balls, buzzed with flies already gathering, and choked with the acrid stench of cordite. He could taste the grit of soil and sweat on his tongue, mixed with the metallic tang of fear.

He saw the enemy line materialize, a blur of gray-clad figures emerging from the smoke, moving with terrifying speed. Bayonets gleamed, fixed for the charge. Silas raised his musket, pulled the trigger, heard the weak click of a misfire. Panic clawed at his throat, colder than any Maine winter. He fumbled again, desperate, his mind screaming. He tried to run, to move, but his legs felt like lead.

Then came the impact. Not the clean shot he'd imagined, but a sickening thud, as if struck by a giant's hammer. He cried out, not in pain, but in sheer animal terror, collapsing into the thorny embrace of a wild blackberry bush. He lay there, tasting dirt and blood, the battle raging over him like a monstrous storm. A musket ball had torn through his left knee, a burning agony, but it was the searing pain in his side, a ripping sensation, that truly stole his breath. He instinctively pressed his hand to it, feeling the wet warmth spread beneath his fingers. Shrapnel.

Through a haze of pain, Silas saw Arthur, his red hair a bright splash of color against the green and brown of the corn. He was still on his feet, grappling hand-to-hand with a Confederate soldier, the two locked in a brutal dance amidst the corn. Arthur fought fiercely, the strength of his blacksmith's arms evident even in the failing light, but another rebel appeared, swinging the butt of his rifle. Arthur went down hard, not silent like Billy, but with a choked cry. The Confederates moved swiftly, dragging him away, deeper into the gathering dusk, leaving only the memory of his thrashing limbs and a desperate, fading call for help. Silas tried to shout, but only a gurgle escaped his bleeding lips.

Silas didn't know how long he lay there. The sounds of fighting slowly receded, replaced by the groans of the wounded, the distant cries of officers, and the terrifying silence of men who would never make another sound. When the stretcher bearers finally found him, the sun had begun to set, painting the blood-soaked cornfield in hues of orange and red. He was alive, patched up in a field hospital, and sent back to his unit. But the war had only just begun its slow, relentless work on him. He stumbled through the carnage of Antietam, the air thick with the metallic tang of blood and the groans of thousands. He shivered through the frozen despair of Fredericksburg, watching men break against stone walls, their lifeblood staining the snow. He slogged through the mud-soaked horror of Chancellorsville, the swampy ground sucking at his boots, the constant, invisible threat of ambush tightening his chest. Each battle peeled back another layer of the man he had been, replacing it with a numbness that spread like frost.

But it was Gettysburg that truly shattered him. Three days of unholy fire and steel, of watching friends fall and the ground turn to churned earth and blood. He stood firm through Pickett's Charge, a living miracle amidst the storm of lead, but by the time the smoke cleared, the victory felt like ashes. The physical wounds from Cedar Mountain had healed, leaving him with a limp and a constant ache, but the wounds Gettysburg inflicted were unseen. The roaring in his ears wasn't just the memory of cannons; it was the screams of the dying, the silent pleas in the eyes of the dead. He returned from Pennsylvania alive, but something fundamental inside him had fractured, leaving a deep, raw wound that no doctor's care could ever mend. The roar of Cedar Mountain, the silent scream of Billy Miller, the chilling image of Arthur Jordan dragged into the darkness—and now the unending, cacophonous symphony of Gettysburg—they would be with him forever.

After Gettysburg, Silas came home to Pondicherry a ghost of his former self. The limp was visible, a constant drag on his left leg, but the true wounds were carried deeper, unseen. He tried to work the small patch of land his family owned, forcing his body through the motions of planting and weeding. But the smell of turned earth sometimes brought back the cloying stench of the battlefield's churned soil and blood, the rhythmic thud of his hoe echoing the sickening thud-thud-thud of falling men. He'd stand in the fields, musket fire roaring in his ears, sweat chilling on his skin even on the hottest July days, his breath catching in his throat.

He couldn't hold a conversation for long. His gaze would drift, unfocusing on the person before him, lost somewhere in the middle distance, and his hands would begin to tremble, sometimes violently, without warning. His jaw would clench, a muscle twitching visibly, as if trying to hold back something terrible. His family, already stretched thin by years of wartime hardship, tried to help. They brought him meals he wouldn't touch, spoke to him in gentle tones he rarely seemed to hear. His mother, her own face pale and drawn, would often sigh, her shoulders slumping a little more each day. But his fits of quiet despair, where he'd sit motionless for hours, turned unpredictably into sudden, unprovoked outbursts—a shouted word, a flung plate, a desperate thrashing in the dark. The nightmares became a constant presence, his screams tearing through the quiet Maine nights, keeping them all awake, leaving them hollow-eyed and helpless in the morning.

There was no understanding for "soldier's heart", no proper medicine for the devils that haunted his mind. The well-meaning whispers of neighbors soon turned to strained silences, then avoidance. Eventually, with no other recourse, and Silas plainly unable to tend to himself, the family, heartbroken but out of options, appealed to the town's Overseers of the Poor. It was Amos Sanborn, the Town Farm Superintendent, who eventually came to fetch him, finding Silas by the silent hearth. He was clutching an unlit pipe, his gaze fixed on the empty grate as if trying to decipher meaning in the dead ashes, utterly lost to the world around him. A faint, almost imperceptible tremor ran through his body even as he sat motionless.

Chapter 5

For decades, Joseph Jakes' days began with the rhythmic thrum of John Perley's mill, his hands calloused from the rough lumber. At home, his wife, Lydia, a woman of tireless motion, spun wool into yarn and kneaded dough, the small farm a testament to their independence. They spoke of the changing seasons, the promise of next year's crop, and the comfort of their routines, never imagining a life beyond their sun-dappled kitchen or the worn path to the mill. Their small house, nestled among the village's familiar rooftops, felt as permanent as the bedrock beneath it. The faint scent of woodsmoke from their hearth mingled with the distant, sweet tang of pine from the mill, a steady perfume of their contented lives.

Then, a sudden, merciless stillness fell over Lydia. One morning, the left side of her body sagged, unresponsive. It was Mrs. Henderson, their next-door neighbor, who found her. She had come over to borrow a cup of sugar, and after knocking twice with no answer, she'd pushed open the unlocked kitchen door. She found Lydia slumped in her rocking chair, her right hand still clutching a half-finished sock, the knitting needles clattering to the floor. Her eyes were open, but distant, and a thin line of drool traced a path from the corner of her mouth. Mrs. Henderson's gasp was a sharp sound in the quiet room. She dropped the sugar bowl, its pewter clatter echoing the sudden fear in her chest.

"Joseph!" Mrs. Henderson shrieked, her voice cracking. She knew where he'd be. Without a second thought, she hiked up her skirts and ran, stumbling down the lane towards the mill, her breath ragged in her throat. She burst through the mill doors, the roar of the machinery momentarily deafening.

"Joseph! Joseph Jakes!" she screamed over the din, pointing wildly back towards his house. "It's Lydia! Something's happened!"

Joseph, covered in sawdust, dropped the timber he was guiding, his face draining of color. The sound of the heavy log hitting the floor was drowned out by the sudden, terrifying silence in his own head. He didn't ask questions. He simply ran, a desperate, stumbling sprint back to his home, his heart hammering against his ribs. He found Lydia exactly as Mrs. Henderson described, his "sweetheart" trapped within her own body. He knelt beside her, murmuring her name, his rough hand stroking her unresponsive cheek.

Within the hour, Dr. Bartlett arrived, his black bag clutched in his hand. He examined Lydia with a somber face, his fingers pressing against her wrist, his ear to her chest. He straightened slowly, shaking his head. "A stroke, Joseph," he said, his voice quiet. "She's paralyzed on her left side. And her speech... it will be a long road, if she recovers it fully." The words hung in the air, heavy and final.

Joseph, his own gait slowed by the years, didn't hesitate. The mill's bell continued to call each dawn, its summons a lifelong habit, but Joseph no longer answered. In those first few days after the stroke, the familiar rhythm of the mill was replaced by the unsettling quiet of their small home. His days became a tender, painstaking dance around Lydia's needs.

He learned the patient art of feeding her, each spoonful a slow, deliberate act. When the fork slipped from her grasp, or a mouthful dribbled down her chin, Joseph, with his gnarled, trembling hands, would gently wipe her face, his touch surprisingly soft. He'd ease his stiff knees to the floor, a low groan escaping him, to clean up spilled broth from the pine boards, the effort a dull ache in his joints.

He helped her shift from bed to chair, his rough hands surprisingly gentle as he guided her weakened limbs, sometimes lifting more of her weight than his own aging frame should bear. "Easy, my girl," he'd murmur, wiping her chin, his gaze unwavering in its devotion. "There you go, sweetheart." His voice, though weary, held an unbreakable tenderness. Every task, however small, was now a monumental effort, a quiet testament to a love that deepened even as their world crumbled around them.

But even as he dedicated himself to Lydia, the weight of the unspoken hung heavy. The mill, his livelihood for decades, called to him not with its bell, but with the chilling silence of lost wages. The decision, though agonizing, was already made.

One crisp morning, Joseph made his way to the mill, not to begin his shift, but to see William Riley, the manager. The familiar scent of sawdust and fresh-cut pine filled his lungs, a bittersweet ache. He found Riley in his office, poring over ledgers, his brow furrowed.

"Morning, William," Joseph said, his voice rougher than usual. He twisted his cap in his hands, unable to meet the younger man's eye. His fingers worried the brim, creasing the worn fabric.

Riley looked up, his face already etched with a knowing concern. "Morning, Joseph. I figured you'd be coming." He put down his pen, his gaze softening. "How is Lydia, truly? We heard about... well, about her stroke."

Joseph cleared his throat, the words catching. "She's... she's not good, William. Needs me. All hours. She can't... she can't manage on her own. And there's no one else." He swallowed hard, the humiliation a bitter taste. "I have to quit, William. I have to care for her."

A long silence settled between them, broken only by the distant, muffled thrum of the mill machinery. William Riley, who had known Joseph his entire life, who had watched him labor with unwavering dedication, saw the defeated slump of the older man's shoulders, the quiet desperation in his averted gaze. He understood the profound, unspoken sacrifice.

"Joseph," Riley said, his voice genuinely empathetic. "I'm truly sorry. For both you and Lydia. You've been the steadiest hand I've ever known, a fixture here. You know this place is always open to you, if things... if things were ever different." He knew they wouldn't be. He also knew that charity, in his business, was a luxury he couldn't often afford.

Joseph finally met Riley's eyes, a fleeting moment of gratitude mixed with the enduring pain of his choice. "I appreciate that, William. You've always been fair." He knew there would be no reprieve, no special arrangement. This was the end of a long, honest working life. He turned to leave, the mill's familiar rumble suddenly sounding like a mournful farewell. The sawdust under his boots felt strangely soft, no longer the firm ground of his purpose.

The silence from the mill, however, soon translated into the chilling silence of unpaid bills. Without Joseph's wages, the carefully balanced scales of their life tipped. The small farm, their pride and their security, became a crushing weight. The sale was swift, brutal in its finality, leaving behind only the echo of lost dreams and a meager purse. The empty house, stripped of their belongings, felt cold even in summer, its silence heavier than any sound.

They retreated to a single room in a Pondicherry boarding house, clinging to the last vestiges of their independence. The landlady's kind smiles soon turned to strained glances as the meager funds dwindled. The crisp banknotes from the farm sale drained away quickly, then vanished, leaving only a hollow emptiness. The smell of stale cooking and too many other bodies in the boarding house replaced the clean air of their farm, pressing in on them.

One Tuesday morning, Joseph, his shoulders bowed, walked a path he had never intended to tread. He avoided eye contact with the few villagers he passed, his face etched with a humiliation deeper than any physical ache. His gaze was fixed on the rough road, as if seeking answers there, or simply trying to disappear. At the selectmen's office, he spoke in a low voice, barely above a whisper, outlining their circumstances, the words catching in his throat like burrs. He did not need to be told the only option remaining.

The news, like a chill wind, swept through Pondicherry. It started as hushed conversations in the general store, then spread to the church steps after Sunday service, and finally, settled over kitchen tables.

"Did you hear about the Jakes?" Mrs. Albright whispered to her neighbor, Mrs. Perkins, as they sorted through bolts of fabric at Knapp & Sanborn's. "Old Joseph and Lydia. Going to the Town Farm, I hear."

Mrs. Perkins paused, her hand hovering over a calico print. "The Jakes? Why, Joseph worked at Perley's mill since before my father's time. Good, honest folk."

"Lydia's stroke, God bless her," Mrs. Albright sighed, shaking her head.

"Joseph stopped work to care for her. Couldn't keep up with the bills, so they say. Lost their farm."

A quiet fell between them, heavier than the unspooling fabric. Mrs. Perkins wrung her hands. "To think. After a lifetime of industry. It just goes to show, doesn't it?" Her gaze drifted out the window, past the familiar storefronts, as if seeing a shadow stretching over her own neat cottage. A shiver ran through her, despite the warmth of the day.

Over at the blacksmith's forge, Leander Frost wiped sweat from his brow, his hammer silent for a moment as he spoke to Thomas Foster. "Heard about old Joseph Jakes. Headed to the Farm with Lydia."

Thomas grunted, tightening a horseshoe. "Aye. A damn shame. Man never took a handout in his life. Always paid his way."

"When the stroke took his wife, he couldn't work. One minute you're providing, the next... you're a burden." Leander kicked at a stray piece of coal on the floor. "Makes a man wonder, don't it? What if it's your back next? Or your wife takes ill?" The heat of the forge suddenly felt less comforting, more like the relentless pressure of life itself. He wiped his hands on his apron, but the worry remained, a cold knot in his stomach.

At the church picnic later that week, even the laughter felt subdued when the Jakes were mentioned. "Such a good couple," Martha Cross murmured to her husband, Cyril, as their children played nearby. "Always so quick to help others."

Cyril nodded, his usual cheer muted. "They lived right, worked hard. Just goes to show you, dear." He glanced at his own children, then back at his wife. "A sudden sickness, a bad turn... and it could be anyone." His voice was low, laced with a fear that echoed in the hearts of many. The Jakes, once just quiet neighbors, now embodied the terrifying fragility of existence in Pondicherry, a living, breathing testament that no matter how hard you worked, how frugal you lived, or how strong your pride, one misstep, one cruel twist of fate, could erase everything and land you at the Town Farm.

Chapter 6

The Pondicherry Town House, a bastion of local democracy, stood on the crest of Main Hill overlooking the town center and the gleaming expanse of Crotched Pond. Built in 1851, it was an impressive structure for its time – though some felt it was already showing its age. It served as a gathering place for all town functions. Today, in the warm air of June 1880, it summoned the men of Pondicherry to their annual town meeting.

Inside, the hall buzzed with a practiced rhythm. Overhead, an impressive arched plaster ceiling added grace and dignity to the otherwise humble proceedings. Rows of hard wooden benches filled quickly, men in their Sunday best or freshly brushed work clothes settling in, their conversations a low hum of gossip, weather, and the ever-present grumbling about taxes. Up on the raised platform, the Selectmen – a sober-faced trio elected to oversee the town's affairs – presided. Among them, undeniably the most imposing figure, was Senator Nat Libby.

He had returned to Pondicherry not long ago, having completed a successful term in Augusta, serving the state senate with the same booming rhetoric he applied to local matters. Yet, in the latest election, he had willingly stepped back into the familiar role of Selectman, and by extension, one of the Overseers of the Poor, a position that allowed him to reconnect with the very heart of the state before his next ascent. His presence on the platform was less a return and more a reassertion of a power he had never truly relinquished in Pondicherry.

Before the meeting officially began, men clustered around him, eager to shake his hand, their voices laced with respect and pride. "Senator!" a portly farmer exclaimed, his hand swallowed by Libby's powerful grip. "Good to have you back in town, sir!"

Libby, a man who savored the deference he commanded, clapped the man's back heartily. "No, no. I'm just a humble Selectman these days, lads. Good to be back." He offered a self-effacing chuckle that was both warm and carefully measured.

"Any truth to the rumor you're running for governor?" another voice called out, laced with a mix of awe and local pride.

Libby's eyes, quick and intelligent, swept over the circle of faces, lingering for just a breath too long on some. "Well, we'll see about that. Plenty of time to think about it." A practiced smile played on his lips.

"You'd do a better job than that idiot up in Augusta right now. That's for sure!" someone else interjected, drawing murmurs of agreement.

Libby laughed, a rich, theatrical sound that filled the small space. "Be that as it may, I'm happy to be back here in Pondicherry serving the town again." His gaze, for a fleeting moment, drifted towards the back of the hall, as if assessing the silent rows, confirming the order he preferred. He adjusted the lapels of his well-tailored coat, a subtle gesture of proprietorship.

The meeting commenced, its early articles gliding smoothly. Appropriations for road repair were approved, schoolhouse maintenance passed without fuss, and the usual levies for town officers were quickly established. The men shifted on their benches, some dozing, others merely enduring the tedium of municipal finance.

Then, the moderator, a reedy man with spectacles perched on his nose, cleared his throat and read aloud:

"Article 11: To see if the Town will vote to raise and appropriate such sums of money as may be necessary for the support of the Poor for the ensuing year, including the maintenance of the Town Farm and the care of such residents of Pondicherry as require residence at the Maine Insane Hospital."

A different kind of tension rippled through the room. This was where the money truly went, where hard-earned taxes disappeared into the bottomless pit of human need. Voices, previously subdued, began to stir. The air, already warm, seemed to thicken, charged with unspoken grievances.

"Another year, another sum bled dry for those unwilling to work!" a gruff voice called out from near the back, immediately drawing nods from several men around him. "My back breaks in my fields, Senator, and I see no reason to foot the bill for idleness!"

"Idleness, indeed," another chimed in, more quietly, a nervous edge to his tone. "But what of the sick, or the orphaned? We can't just turn them out." There was a collective murmur of agreement; Pondicherry, like any small town, held onto a shred of Christian charity, a sense that some misfortune was simply unavoidable. The Town Farm, for many, was a necessary evil – a grim but unavoidable part of maintaining communal order, a last resort for lives broken beyond mending.

But others harbored a different resentment. "And is it even run properly?" demanded a sharp, clipped voice from the middle of the room, belonging to a shopkeeper known for his meticulous ledgers. "I hear tell of expenses that don't quite add up. We're paying to keep that place, but are we getting our money's worth? Perhaps a tighter hand is needed." This criticism was often whispered in the barber shop and the general store: the Farm was a drain, and perhaps its inefficiencies made it more so.

Beneath the overt complaints and the grumbling, an unspoken fear threaded through the hall, a phantom chill on the June air. Every man present, from the prosperous farmer to the struggling mill worker, knew the precariousness of life. A bad harvest, an accident in the quarry, a sudden illness, a death in the family – any one of these could unravel a man's fortunes, could leave his wife a widow, his children destitute. The Town Farm, standing bleakly on the edge of their community, was a stark, ever-present reminder of how thin the line truly was between respectability and ruin. It was a place where "us" could become "them" with terrifying swiftness, a fate they vehemently wished to avoid, even as they debated the cost of its upkeep.

The murmuring grew louder, threatening to break into more direct argument. Sensing the shift, Libby leaned forward further, his gaze sweeping the room, preparing to guide the volatile sentiments into channels that served his purpose. His experience in Augusta had honed his ability to tame a room, to manipulate fears and direct loyalties. And he had very specific ideas about how the poor of Pondicherry should be managed.

Libby's smile, imperceptible to most, widened slightly as the grumbling intensified. This was his element – the cacophony of public opinion, ripe for shaping. He cleared his throat, a sound remarkably quiet for its immediate effect. The murmurs died down, attention snapping to the platform.

"Gentlemen," he began, his voice dropping to a confidential tone that somehow carried to every corner of the room, "I understand your concerns. Believe me, having spent my recent years in Augusta, witnessing the profligacy of certain state expenditures, I share your vigilance. No man works harder for his dollar than the good people of Pondicherry, and it pains me to see any of it wasted."

He paused, letting the words sink in, allowing a collective sigh of agreement to ripple through the room.

"The Town Farm," he continued, now adopting a more serious, almost somber register, "is indeed a necessary burden. A Christian community must care for its truly unfortunate. But it must be run with the same prudence and industry we expect in our own homes and farms." His gaze swept across the benches, pausing here and there, making individual men feel personally addressed. "And I agree, there are inefficiencies that, as an Overseer of the Poor, I intend to address with a firm hand."

A few approving nods could be seen. He had successfully steered the conversation from abstract resentment to a shared, actionable concern for efficiency, subtly validating the complaints.

"However," Libby's voice deepened, his eyes now seeming to bore into the very pockets of the taxpayers, "let us consider where our truly exorbitant expenditures lie. We send certain... difficult cases to the Maine Insane Hospital. A necessary measure, perhaps, for those beyond our local capacity, but let us examine the cost."

He held up a hand, preventing immediate interjections. "I have reviewed the figures. For a single individual residing at the State Hospital, Pondicherry is bled for sums that could support three, perhaps even four, paupers here at our own Town Farm. Four souls, gentlemen! For the price of one difficult case in Augusta, we could provide for multiple local unfortunates, right here in our own community, where their care can be... overseen more directly."

His emphasis on "overseen directly" was subtle but clear, hinting at control beyond mere fiscal management. He let the stark numbers hang in the air, allowing the men to perform the mental arithmetic. Four for one. The argument was, on its surface, irrefutable for a tax-conscious town.

"We have individuals, here in Pondicherry," Libby continued, his voice lowering almost to a conspiratorial whisper, "who, while presenting considerable challenges, do not necessarily require the entirety of the state's resources. Individuals who, with careful management and the proper facilities—which we can, and indeed must, ensure at our own Farm—could be contained locally, and at a fraction of the cost to you, the honest, hardworking taxpayers."

He didn't name Harriet Woodbury. He didn't have to. The unspoken implication hung heavy in the air, a silent agreement forming in the room. Why pay a king's ransom to house a dangerous lunatic far away when she could be contained at the Farm, cheaply and effectively, solving two problems at once: draining the town's coffers less, and ensuring Pondicherry's difficulties remained Pondicherry's alone. Libby's gaze, unblinking, surveyed the room, confirming he had captured their assent. He knew a few, like Josiah Croft, would balk, but the overwhelming sentiment, fueled by fear and disdain of the poor and the specter of their own potential ruin, was now firmly on his side.

As the crisp autumn air deepened into the biting chill of December, the ominous undertones of the selectmen's meeting did not touch the inmates of the Pondicherry Town Farm. For them, the approaching Christmas brought a rare ripple of anticipation. The Pondicherry Village Church, under the gentle guidance of Reverend William Hague, was preparing for its annual Christmas gathering. Reverend Hague was known for his quiet kindness and his belief that even the humblest souls deserved a moment of grace and joy. His approach was a welcome balm after the stern hand of the previous

Pastor, Holland B. Frye, a Civil War veteran whose austere discipline mirrored the battlefields he'd known. Pastor Frye, who had banned all concerts and entertainments from the church vestry, insisting only on purely religious events, was still vividly remembered by the town's young people, whose fierce resentment had famously led them to hang his portrait in the "indoor outhouse" upon his departure.

The church now buzzed with a simpler, warmer spirit under Reverend Hague. For Edwin, even a brief escape from the farm, a chance to see the village lights and faces, held its own quiet allure.

On Christmas Eve, the inmates able to leave the farm were cleaned up, dressed in their best (though still patched and worn) clothes, and loaded into the wagon for the short journey to the church. The air was sharp and clean, carrying the distant scent of woodsmoke and crisp pine. Inside the church, the warmth radiating from the pot-bellied stoves and the soft murmur of voices were a stark, welcome contrast to the perpetual chill and silence of the farm. Edwin found a seat with the other inmates, under the ever-watchful, though gentle, eye of Marylou. She sat among them, a quiet anchor, her presence a familiar comfort. For Marylou, too, the church offered a momentary reprieve from the relentless duties of the farm, a whisper of the community life she once knew, before Abraham was lost and her own home was just a memory. She smoothed the worn fabric of her own dress, a faint ache in her chest for lost warmth.

The service began. The choir, their voices a soft, reverent harmony, opened with "Away in a Manger," its simple melody filling the old wooden beams. As the verses unfolded, Edwin caught sight of Mrs. Lewis among the choir members. Her voice, a steady harmony, blended with the others. For a brief moment, her gaze found his across the crowded pews, and she offered him a small, kind smile—a rare, gentle acknowledgment that made him feel seen, if only for a second. This was followed by hymns, their familiar tunes now sung by the full congregation, then Reverend Hague's sermon, a comforting message of peace and goodwill. Edwin, usually restless during long sittings, found a quiet contentment in the collective warmth. Afterward came the moment for the distribution of gifts, a modest affair overseen by the Reverend himself. Small, practical items were handed out to the needy from the town, along with simple treats. Edwin received a new pair of coarse wool socks, still smelling faintly of sheep, and a single, perfectly ripe orange – its bright color and sweet, tangy scent a rare and precious luxury that tasted of freedom and an outside world he barely knew. He held the orange carefully in his palm, its smooth, cool skin a stark contrast to the rough wool of his new socks.

As the inmates were gathered to return to the wagon, Edwin caught sight of Mrs. Lewis again, now busy near the front pews, directing volunteers in the cleanup with precise movements and a quiet, commanding spirit. Her gaze swept over the departing inmates, lingering, Edwin felt, on him for just a moment longer than on the others. He returned her brief, kind smile, clutching his orange. He saw her now exchange a quiet, knowing look with Marylou, a quick, almost imperceptible nod passing between them before Marylou ushered the last of the inmates towards the door. The simple act of kindness, the warmth of the church, and the rare, citrus-bright taste of the orange clung to Edwin, a fleeting ember against the lengthening shadow of winter, long after the last glow of the church candles vanished from sight. He imagined the warmth of the church, a bulwark against the cold on the dark ride to the Farm. The memory of Mrs. Lewis's smile, too, seemed to hold a small, internal heat.

Chapter 7

The winter of 1881 settled over Pondicherry with a familiar, biting intensity. January winds howled across the ponds and lakes, scoured the exposed fields, and rattled the worn windows of the Town Farm. The short, gray days bled into long, brutal nights, and the inmates huddled closer to the cast-iron stove, drawing meager comfort from its warmth. The rhythms of the farm grew slower, deeper, a hushed struggle against the cold, punctuated only by the lowing of cattle and the creak of ice underfoot. But this winter, a new and unsettling chill was about to descend.

One frigid afternoon, a sleigh pulled up to the main door, its runners crunching loudly on the frozen snow. It wasn't the doctor, nor a delivery from the general store. Instead, Squire Nat Libby himself emerged, his breath pluming in the icy air, accompanied by another selectman, Thomas Albright. Mr. Sanborn, emerging from the barn, looked at his wife, Dorcas, who stood framed in the doorway, a look of immediate concern clouding her face. She always seemed to sense bad news before it spoke.

Libby, stamping snow from his boots in the mudroom, wasted no time on pleasantries. "Sanborn," he boomed, his voice echoing in the small space, "the Town has made its decision regarding the Woodbury woman. She'll be transferred to the Farm by the end of the week."

Dorcas Sanborn gasped, a soft, involuntary sound. Her hand went to her mouth, her eyes wide with dismay. "H-h-harriet Woodbury? But, Senator, she's... she's quite unmanageable. The Hospital—"

"The Hospital is a drain on the town's purse, Mrs. Sanborn," Libby cut her off, his tone losing its public charm, hardening to a definitive edge.

"Pondicherry taxpayers will no longer foot such an exorbitant bill for a single, difficult soul. She'll be contained here, where she can be properly looked after, and far more economically. The decision was made at the Town Meeting. It is settled."

Mr. Sanborn merely nodded, his face etched with a weary resignation that spoke volumes. He knew better than to argue with Libby once a decision was made, especially one that came with the full weight of a town vote. But Dorcas continued to look distraught, her gaze drifting back towards the warmth of the kitchen where Nan sat working on her schoolwork. Nan. Dear God.

Edwin, fetching wood for the kitchen stove, had been drawn by the arrival. He saw Nan, ten-year-old daughter of the Sanborns, peeking around the corner from the warmth of the kitchen, her small face pale. Her eyes, wide and luminous, met Edwin's, mirroring his own dawning dread. They knew the whispers about Harriet Woodbury – the "idiotic, insane" woman, the "danger." They'd heard the adults speak in hushed, fearful tones of her outbursts, her strength. The idea of such a person being brought here, to their home, sent a shiver down Nan's spine that Edwin could almost feel. She clutched his arm, her small fingers digging in. "They say she's a dangerous lunatic," she whispered, the words echoing their shared childhood terror.

The concern wasn't limited to the children. Throughout the farm, a palpable unease spread among the inmates. Joseph Jakes, seated by the dining room window, shared a grave, knowing look with his wife, Lydia, whose frail hand instinctively reached for his. Silas Andrews, whittling by the stove, paused, his knife still, his gaze fixed on nothing. Marylou, usually bustling in the kitchen, leaned heavily against the counter, her normally energetic movements stilled by a sudden, heavy quiet. A cold dread seeped into her bones, familiar from other losses. They all understood. Their precarious sanctuary was about to be breached by something truly volatile, something that would demand more space, more fear, more control.

Within days, the peace of the frozen farm was shattered by the clang of hammers and the rasp of saws. Men from town, contracted by the Selectmen, arrived with lumber and iron, setting to work in a storage room in the ell. The sounds were jarring, discordant, violating the quiet domesticity that the

Sanborns had managed to maintain. Walls were reinforced, thick planks fitted together, and finally, a formidable gate of iron bars was installed, forming a cage within the farm walls. It was stark, cruel, and undeniably secure. The air itself seemed to vibrate with the percussive blows, a grim sign of impending confinement.

The entire process created a strange, foreboding atmosphere that seeped into every corner of the Town Farm. The very air seemed to thicken with dread, the usual daily tasks now performed under the shadow of the looming cage. It felt less like a home and more like a prison, its purpose no longer just to house the unfortunate, but to contain the uncontainable.

And then, one bitterly cold afternoon, the new presence arrived. A covered wagon, even larger than the previous sleigh, rumbled up the drive, its heavy springs groaning under an unseen weight. Edwin, along with Nan, watched from the window as the men emerged, carrying a bundled, struggling form into the ell. Harriet Woodbury had arrived.

The moment Harriet Woodbury was carried into the ell, the foreboding atmosphere that had settled over the farm curdled into terror. The men who had brought her vanished quickly, leaving behind only the cold, the snow, and the chilling echoes of a presence now firmly entrenched within the Farm's walls.

That first night, January unleashed its full fury. The wind, a living, howling beast, tore at the eaves, its mournful cry seeming to seep through every crack in the old building. Windows in their ill-fitting frames rattled incessantly, a percussive backdrop to the nightmare unfolding in the ell.

From Harriet Woodbury's cage, the sounds began. Not human cries, not even animalistic growls, but something in between – guttural screeches that scraped against the very marrow of bone, punctuated by the metallic clang and shudder of the iron bars. She hammered against them, seemingly tirelessly, with a strength born of pure, desperate madness. Each impact sent a dull thud through the very foundation of the building, a sickening pulse of contained fury. The rattling, a relentless, jarring rhythm, reverberated through the connecting walls of the Farm, a constant reminder that the uncontainable had indeed been contained, but not subdued.

Edwin lay in his cot, eyes wide open in the absolute darkness, every nerve vibrating with the sounds. The wind outside seemed to amplify her cries, weaving them into a terrifying symphony of winter and madness. He sensed Wesley trembling in the cot next to his, already agitated by the howling wind, unable to understand the new noises. Nan, frightened, left her room and climbed into her parent's bed, her small body curled into a tight knot against them, her breath coming in shallow, ragged gasps.

Through the thin walls, the other inmates tossed and turned. Joseph Jakes coughed more frequently, a dry, anxious sound, and Lydia's soft moans seemed to rise in response to Harriet's screeches. Silas Andrews could be heard pacing all night, a restless shadow in his room on the second floor. From a small, shadowed cot, Jane Small whimpered, clutching her worn dolly close, the only comfort against the panic that tightened its grip around her fragile heart. She had known the stark halls of the Maine Insane Hospital, the rampant fear, and now here, the fear in the air was a palpable thing. The usual low snores and gentle breathing of a sleeping household were replaced by a tense, strained silence, occasionally broken by a frightened whisper or a stifled sob.

In their own small quarters, Mr. and Mrs. Sanborn lay awake, their faces illuminated by the flickering light of a single oil lamp. Dorcas pressed her hands over her ears, her eyes shut tight, but the sounds still seemed to pierce through. Mr. Sanborn, jaw set, stared at the ceiling, the full weight of Libby's decision, and the dangerous burden it had thrust upon his Farm, heavy on his shoulders. Dorcas had been right to worry; her premonition had come to a horrific fruition. She brought poor, frightened Nan into their bed and tucked her small frame under her protective arm.

The night stretched on, endless and terrifying. Harriet Woodbury's screeches, the clang of her cage, and the relentless howl of the January wind filled the darkness. At last, just before dawn, the wind died down and Harriet Woodbury fell silent.

Chapter 8

Harriet Woodbury's first night at the Town Farm bled into weeks, then months, painting the harsh Maine winter with a new, terrifying shade. Her screeches, the clang of iron bars, and the ceaseless, desperate struggle against her confinement became the Farm's brutal new rhythm. The initial shock curdled into a pervasive dread, a constant tremor beneath the thin veneer of daily life. The ell, once just a collection of storage rooms, now felt like the Farm's dark, beating heart, thrumming with raw madness.

For Dorcas Sanborn, the incessant torment was agonizing. Every jarring clang, every guttural shriek, seemed to pierce not just the walls, but her very soul. More than her own discomfort, however, it was the effect on Nan that tore at her. Her daughter had been stripped of her easy laughter, replaced by a nervous jumpiness and a haunting pallor. Nan still sought the comfort of her parents' bed on the worst nights, but even in the shared warmth, Dorcas could feel the tremor of fear that never quite left the child's small frame. Was this to be Nan's girlhood? To grow into young womanhood with the constant, terrifying presence of a "crazed, dangerous lunatic" in the next wing? The thought twisted in Dorcas's gut, a knot of sickening dread.

She spoke of it often to Mr. Sanborn in the quiet, flickering lamplight of their private quarters, her voice low so it wouldn't carry through the thin walls. "Amos, we can't stay. Not like this. Not with Nan. What kind of life is this for her?"

Mr. Sanborn, weary from his duties and the new, heavy burden of supervision, would sigh, running a hand over his thinning hair. "It's our duty, Dorcas. We took the contract."

"And what of our duty to our own child?" she would counter, her voice tight with suppressed desperation. "She's not meant for this, Amos. None of us are. But for her, it is formative. Do we want her growing up with the screams of a madwoman as her lullaby? With a cage for a neighbor? She deserves the quiet chirp of crickets, the rustle of leaves, not this awful, clanging din."

The discussions continued through February and into March, growing more frequent, more strained. Their contract was up for renewal in April, and the decision weighed on them like the winter snow on the barn roof. They loved the farm in its own way, had built a life there, offered what meager kindness they could to the unfortunates placed in their charge. Leaving felt like an abandonment, a failure of their commitment. But the vision of Nan, bright and sensitive, slowly wilting under the oppressive atmosphere, haunted Dorcas. It was a wrenching choice, duty battling parental love.

Unbeknownst to the Sanborns, their conflicted deliberations were exactly the opportunity Nat Libby had been waiting for. When word of their uncertainty, however subtle, reached the Selectmen, Libby pounced. He convened a special meeting of the Overseers of the Poor, his arguments precise and cutting. The Town Farm, he declared, needed a firmer hand. It needed a superintendent who would prioritize efficiency above all else, one who understood the necessity of strict discipline and rigorous regimens, particularly now with more challenging cases like Harriet. The Sanborns, while well-meaning, were perhaps too... soft for the task ahead. He articulated his points with an almost surgical precision, each word a chisel shaping their agreement. He knew just the man.

Philemon Flint, a gaunt, unsmiling figure from upcountry, had a fearsome reputation as a manager of lumber camps and, more recently, a smaller, notoriously strict poorhouse in a neighboring county. He was a man steeped in a harsh, puritanical brand of faith, convinced that idleness was the devil's workshop and that suffering, meted out with stern discipline, was the only path to moral rectitude. Punishment was not just a deterrent; it was a cleansing. The Selectmen, swayed by Libby's rhetoric and the promise of lower expenditures, quickly agreed. Flint was exactly what Pondicherry needed, they concluded, to finally bring the unruly poor to heel.

The news was delivered to the Sanborns in mid-March: a new superinten-dent had been chosen. Their contract would not be renewed. A strange mix of relief and sorrow washed over them. The decision had been made for them, and though it stung their pride, it cleared the path for Nan's escape. They would return to their small home farm, a patch of land Amos had inherited, less demanding, more peaceful. Better for Nan.

As the days dwindled towards April, a sense of quiet desperation settled over the Farm, particularly for Edwin. He saw the Sanborns' trunks being packed, felt Nan's increasing distance as she embraced the idea of a new life. On their last night, a palpable ache settled in his chest. He had no gift to offer Nan, no store-bought trinket. But for weeks, he had been carving, patiently shaping a piece of smooth maple wood with his crude knife. It was a small bird, caught mid-flight, its wings spread as if about to soar free. Awkwardly, he pressed it into Nan's hand. "For luck," he mumbled, his throat tight. "So you remember."

Nan's eyes welled, but she nodded fiercely, clutching the bird. The next morning, just before the Sanborns climbed into their wagon, Nan pressed something into Edwin's hand. It was a handkerchief, neatly folded, made of fine, soft cotton. Embroidered in one corner, with tiny, imperfect stitches, were the letters: E.L. "So you remember," she whispered, her voice choked with tears. "It's... it's just for you."

Edwin stared at it, a wave of unfamiliar emotion washing over him. A handkerchief. Monogrammed. For him. It was the first item he had ever owned that was made specifically for him, that acknowledged him as a person important enough to have such a (to him) fancy item. It was a tangible mark of his existence, a recognition from someone who truly saw him. A warmth spread through his palm from the cloth, a feeling entirely new, akin to the sun after a long winter. He didn't know what to say. Later, when the Farm had fallen silent after the Sanborns' departure, Edwin tucked the handkerchief carefully under his thin straw pillow, a secret comfort in a suddenly colder world.

Philemon Flint arrived the following day, a gaunt shadow against the spring light, his wife trailing silently behind him. He wasted no time. The first thing he did was gather the inmates, his voice a low, gravelly rasp that promised no kindness. He spoke of God's wrath, of the virtues of hard labor, of cleansing the soul through rigorous routine. There would be no more "coddling." Every inmate would earn their keep. The air in the keeping room seemed to grow heavier, colder, with his every pronouncement. A faint, unpleasant scent of stale tobacco and unwashed wool seemed to emanate from him, clinging to the space like a shroud.

Chapter 9

The Town Farm, once a haven of ordered quiet under the Sanborns, transformed into a crucible under Philemon Flint. The very air seemed to crackle with his rigid interpretation of faith and duty, a philosophy that saw idleness as sin and suffering as a path to salvation. His rule was absolute, driven by the mandate from the Selectmen – a relentless pursuit of economy and efficiency, achieved at the staggering expense of human dignity.

For Harriet Woodbury, Flint's arrival marked the descent into a deeper hell. Her madness, far from eliciting pity, was to him a manifestation of a soul in need of purging, a stubborn spirit requiring forceful correction. Almost daily, the sound of water splashing from the kitchen pump would precede the ominous clatter of a tin tub being dragged into the ell. Then came Flint's gravelly commands, punctuated by Harriet's rising, terrified wails.

Edwin, working nearby, would hear the splash, the gasp, the thrashing, followed by a torrent of guttural screeches that were no longer just random outbursts, but sounds of deliberate, intense pain. The frigid water, meant not to soothe but to shock, forced the breath from her lungs. She would shiver violently, her limbs flailing against the sides of the tub, against the very air, as if trying to escape an invisible tormentor. Flint would stand over her, grim-faced, sometimes holding her down, convinced he was scrubbing the madness from her very essence. Her cries, raw and desperate, now took on a new, consistent quality, a tortured protest against this deliberate torment. They became a part of the Farm's daily soundscape, a chilling reminder of Flint's "discipline."

Silas Andrews, a man whose quiet moments and haunted gaze marked him as grappling with unseen demons, quickly drew Flint's ire. Flint saw the tremor in Silas's hand, the way his eyes would sometimes glaze over and fix on some distant, unseen horror, not as an affliction but as a blatant attempt to feign illness and shirk work. "Laziness masquerading as melancholy!" Flint would bellow, his voice like stones grinding together. "There's no room for such indulgence here. God grants strength to those willing to use it."

Silas was assigned the most brutal, repetitive tasks – endlessly chopping firewood into precise lengths, hauling stones from the fields until his shoulders ached with a dull, persistent fire. Flint would stand over him, a dark, looming shadow, sometimes striking a log a sharp blow with his own axe to underscore the pace he expected. If Silas paused, lost for a moment in the vacant stare that meant his mind had retreated, Flint would bark, "Move! Or do you expect charity for your idleness?" The threat of reduced rations hung unspoken in the air, a chilling reminder that work was the only currency accepted. Silas grew gaunt, his eyes receding into hollow sockets, but the ceaseless labor permitted no escape. He moved like a puppet on fraying strings, his body obeying while his mind floated somewhere else, a fragile protection.

Upstairs, in the small room under the eaves, Ned Lakin endured a different kind of torment. Flint, true to his word, saw Ned's crippled leg not as a permanent injury but as a convenient excuse. The small stack of books by Ned's cot, once a lifeline to other worlds, were removed as Flint dismissed reading novels as "profligate nonsense." He'd stride into the room, his heavy boots echoing on the floor, and cast a withering glance at Ned. "Still abed, boy? A man's worth is in his labor, not in the idle dreams he spins from paper. Get up, or you'll find your rations reflect your contributions!" He wouldn't offer a hand, wouldn't suggest a task Ned could manage from his cot, simply leaving the threat hanging in the air, a constant pressure on Ned's already fragile spirit. The unspoken message was clear: Ned was a drain, a useless mouth, and Flint's contempt hung over him like the stifling summer heat. Ned often pulled his thin blanket higher, not just from cold, but from the invisible weight of Flint's disapproval.

Edwin, strong and able-bodied, found himself the primary engine of Flint's drive for efficiency. Dawn broke, and Edwin was already in the fields, his breath pluming in the cold, hands raw on the plow. He hauled stones until his back screamed, chopped wood until his arms burned, and performed every chore Flint could invent, from mending fences in the biting wind to mucking out the deepest stalls. His young muscles strained, knotted with fatigue that never fully receded. Each day melted into the next in a haze of relentless labor, demanding his strength from before dawn until well after dusk. Flint's eyes, sharp and calculating, followed him, always seeking another task, another ounce of utility to extract. There was no praise, no respite, only the unspoken expectation of endless output. It was containment through exhaustion, a deliberate attempt to break his spirit through sheer physical burden, to leave him too weary to think, too tired to dream of anything beyond the next moment of rest. Even the air he breathed felt heavy, thick with the unspoken command to work, to produce, until he was empty.

The aged inmates suffered most quietly, their decline a hushed tragedy in the corners of the Farm. Joseph and Lydia Jakes, with their hacking coughs and the increasingly pained shuffling of their feet, began to fade with alarming speed. Lydia's breathing grew shallow, punctuated by gasping efforts that left her chest heaving. Joseph's movements became stiff, each rise from a chair a slow, agonizing process. They barely ate, the coarse rations offering little sustenance for their failing bodies. Their pleas for help, whispered to Marylou in moments of desperate hope, met with Flint's unyielding refusal. Dr. Bartlett, the town physician, was a name Flint dismissed with a wave of his hand, a costly, unnecessary extravagance. "God provides," Flint would intone, his voice devoid of sympathy, "or He takes. We are not to interfere with His will through profligate spending on the unproductive. Their time is in His hands." The Jakes were left to suffer, their cries for comfort unheard, their bodies slowly succumbing to neglect, becoming little more than shadows on the dining room benches.

Mrs. Flint, a silent shadow to her husband's austere presence, often found herself at a loss for how to manage Harriet's relentless agitation. The constant screeches wore at her nerves, fraying the strained quiet of her new home. Then, one dreary afternoon, the Farm lane stirred with an uncharacteristic flash of color. A lively wagon, painted with bold claims and adorned with bright, optimistic lettering, pulled up. From it sprang a traveling patent medicine man. He was a man all smiles and glib promises, his breath smelling of peppermint and cheap spirits, his pockets jingling with bottles.

He greeted Mrs. Flint with a flourish, his eyes quickly assessing her weary face. "Madam," he declared, pulling a small, corked bottle from his sample bag, "I perceive a spirit troubled by... agitating influences." He paused for dramatic effect. "May I introduce to you *Dr. Godfrey's Cordial!* A soothing syrup, madam, made from nature's purest herbs, perfect for calming nervous dispositions, for ensuring peaceful repose, for bringing tranquility where turmoil reigns." He held up the bottle, its label featuring a serene, almost angelic, child. Its fancy name and innocuous description concealed its true, potent ingredient: laudanum, a powerful opiate. Mrs. Flint, desperate for any reprieve from Harriet's screams, saw not a potential danger, but a miracle in a bottle. She readily purchased a large one.

She began dosing Harriet, a small spoonful mixed into her thin, unappetizing gruel. For a time, it seemed to work. The guttural screeches lessened, replaced by a heavy, drugged quiet. To Mrs. Flint, it was a blessing, a fragile peace won from chaos. But one day, a minor crisis erupted in the kitchen — a sudden, piercing shriek from Marylou as she sliced her hand deeply while cutting slabs of bacon. Mrs. Flint, flustered and distracted, rushed to attend to it, leaving the nearly-full bottle of "Cordial" on a small table in the ell, dangerously close to the iron bars of Harriet's cage.

A sudden, chilling quiet fell over the ell, a silence more profound than any peace the laudanum had offered. In a rare, perhaps fleeting moment of terrible lucidity, or driven by a sudden, desperate instinct for escape from her torment, Harriet reached out. Her fingers, surprisingly nimble despite her emaciated frame, closed around the cool glass. With a primal, guttural sound, a sound of profound desperation, she brought the bottle to her lips. In one rapid, unthinking motion, she tipped it back, swallowing the entire remaining contents. The dark liquid vanished down her throat, leaving only a few tell-tale drops clinging to the empty bottle.

The unnatural silence lingered. Later that evening, as twilight deepened,

Marylou, arriving with Harriet's meager dinner, was the one who found her: still and cold, the empty bottle of *Dr. Godfrey's Cordial* clutched loosely in her lifeless hand. Marylou, a woman who had known too much death, from her Abraham on a Civil War battlefield to the slow fading of countless inmates, felt a familiar ache, but this was different. Her heart, already heavy with grief for Harriet's torments, now swelled with a burning indignation. She knew about treating minor ailments, about the careful measure of tonics, and the sheer recklessness of leaving such a potent brew within reach of a desperate soul. A tremor ran through her, not of fear, but of righteous fury, coiling tight in her gut.

Driven by a deep-seated sense of justice and her quiet, fierce promise to Edwin's mother to look after the boy, she could not hold her tongue. She stormed from the ell, confronting Prudence Flint in the kitchen, her voice low but unwavering, though laced with furious accusation. "You left it, ma'am. You left the bottle right there. You killed her."

Prudence Flint, pale and shaken by Marylou's raw fury and the damning truth in her words, immediately fetched her husband. Philemon Flint's face darkened, his eyes narrowing to slits. "You overstep, woman! Such slander will not be tolerated." There was no denial, no attempt to explain, only a furious defense of his authority, a desperate attempt to silence the truth with bluster. He dismissed her on the spot. "You are no longer welcome here. Gather your things and be gone by sundown!"

It was a sad parting. Marylou found herself cast out from the only semblance of stability she had. She clutched Edwin fiercely, her eyes brimming. "Be strong, boy," she whispered, her voice thick. "Hold fast." She desperately wanted to stay, to honor her vow, to be a shield against the rising tide of Flint's cruelty, but she had no choice. The power of the superintendent, backed by the Selectmen, was absolute. With her small pension barely a whisper of security and her sons so far away, her own existence threatened, Marylou had no choice but to turn her back and walk away, leaving Edwin utterly alone amongst the escalating harshness.

Chapter 10

The sudden, unnatural silence from the ell hung heavy over the Town Farm, a chilling testament to Harriet Woodbury's final, desperate act. For Philemon and Prudence Flint, however, that silence was less a blessing and more a hammer blow of terror. Shocked and disbelieving, their first, panicked thought wasn't of Harriet's suffering, but of their own precarious livelihood. Should the truth of her death—the haphazard dosing, the neglected bottle—come to light, their tenure, their very reputation, would be ruined.

Under the shroud of a moonless night, the only sound was the hurried, rhythmic scrape of a shovel against frozen earth. Philemon Flint stood over Edwin, a silent, menacing shadow, watching as the boy dug, his breath pluming in the frigid air. Prudence Flint stood by, a silent, shivering sentinel, her face a pale blur in the gloom. Harriet Woodbury's body, still and slight beneath a rough, homespun sheet, offered no resistance. Edwin plunged the shovel again and again into the hard ground of the burial plot. He knew this desolate patch beyond the apple orchard, marked only by a few neglected, nameless mounds, was where the forgotten dead of the Town Farm lay. And somewhere within it, beneath his very feet, lay his own mother, as nameless and forgotten to the world as the woman he now buried. There was no minister, no whispered prayer, no last rite to consecrate the meager parcel of earth. Just the urgent need to conceal. The earth, hard and resistant with the lingering grip of winter, fought Edwin's efforts, but Flint's looming presence and their desperate fear drove him on, burying their terrible secret along with the woman. The chill of the night seemed to seep into his very bones, a cold that had nothing to do with the weather.

Days later, a terse, official report landed on the desk of the Overseers of the Poor. Harriet Woodbury, it stated, had "passed away quietly in her sleep, a release from her earthly torments." Philemon Flint, when questioned, modulated his voice to a tone of carefully constructed solemnity. "A blessing, poor dear," he intoned, his gaze fixed somewhere beyond his questioner's face, "she found her peace at last." The words were chosen with precision, a narrative crafted to close the book on a difficult, costly case. And in a final, chilling note of his enduring dedication to economy, the report concluded with a request for reimbursement for the cost of a pine coffin—a coffin that, like Harriet's dignity, was never provided.

But despite the Flints' desperate secrecy, the inmates all knew. They had heard the muffled sounds of the digging, noted the sudden, profound quiet in the ell that was far too deep to be natural, seen the Flints' tight, wary faces and their hasty, furtive movements. They'd seen the shovel, leaning freshly scraped against the barn wall at dawn, or caught the faint scent of disturbed earth on the cold air. A silent, shared knowledge of the truth settled among them, hardening their fear into a bitter, resentful understanding.

The quiet despair that had settled over the Farm after Harriet's death, a heavy blanket of fear and submission, was abruptly shattered by another, more public crisis. Wesley, fragile and constantly agitated, had been pushed to his breaking point. The sounds from the ell had terrified him, and he'd witnessed Flint's casual brutality firsthand—the swift, unprovoked blows, the chilling, righteous anger in the man's eyes. He flinched at every raised voice, every sudden movement. His body had become a tightly wound spring, ready to recoil at the slightest provocation. His small, already fractured world tightened with unbearable dread, a dread that culminated one bitter morning.

Wesley failed to complete a chore to Flint's exacting, impossible standard, and the superintendent's heavy hand descended. The sound of the beating, dull thuds followed by Wesley's whimpers, echoed in the barn. When Flint finally stalked away, Wesley lay shaking and whimpering. Edwin and Silas wiped the tears and snot from his face, and helped him to his room.

The next morning, Matron's sharp query cut through the usual breakfast din. "Where's Wesley?" Edwin, who hadn't seen the boy since helping him to bed, could only shake his head. "I don't know, Ma'am. He was already up before me." A look of concern crossed Matron's face. "Run out and see if he's in the privy or the barn."

Edwin raced out, worried for his friend. The privy door hung open, empty. He ran for the barn. Bessie greeted him with a mournful low. The horses gave a friendly nicker. No Wesley. He called for him, his voice echoing in the vast space. No answer. He climbed the ladder to the haymow, hoping to find Wesley asleep there as he sometimes liked to do. Empty. He flung himself down the ladder, racing across the barnyard. "Wesley! Wesley!" His shouts bounced back, swallowed by the cold morning air.

The kitchen door burst open, and Flint's furious face appeared. "Where'd that little idiot get to?" He grabbed Edwin by the collar, his grip tight enough to choke. "I don't know, Sir." Flint gave him a violent shove. "Run to get Cyril Cross. Tell him the idiot's escaped!"

The alarm screamed across the farmyard. Shouts carried, and the chilling news of Wesley's disappearance spread like wildfire, igniting a desperate scramble. Search parties, a mix of farmhands and concerned neighbors already uneasy with the grim rumors from the Town Farm, immediately fanned out, plunging into the bitter cold. Lanterns bobbed in the pre-dawn gloom, their beams slicing through swirling mist as they combed frozen woods and icy fields. Edwin, his own heart a cold knot of dread, knew the boy's terror and the familiar contours of the local terrain. He pushed himself, fueled by the desperate hope of finding Wesley before the brutal cold claimed him, shouting the boy's name until his throat was raw. As the sun rose higher, more town members joined the search, their faces etched with deepening concern.

Whispers of Flint's harshness, once confined to hushed corners, now erupted into open condemnation. Many knew Wesley, if only vaguely, as the great-grandson of one of the town's founding fathers, a lineage that lent a surprising weight to his plight. The idea that a member, however distant, of such a prominent family could be so ill-treated, spurred a rising tide of anger among the more respectable citizens. It was talked about at the general store, in quiet, disapproving tones. It was discussed in hushed, somber conversations after church, over coffee and doughnuts, the grim details spreading from adult to adult. Even school children whispered about it on the playground, their games momentarily forgotten as they exchanged fearful rumors. The outrage was a slow-burning fire that finally found enough air to blaze, fueled by Wesley's lineage and the unbearable thought that such cruelty could touch anyone, even indirectly.

After an extensive search that stretched into a second grueling day through the frigid woods and along the winding streams, it was Silas and Edwin who finally found him. They discovered Wesley shivering violently, huddled on the cold, muddy banks of Peabody Pond, a couple of miles from the Farm. He was alive, but barely, his body chilled to the bone, his mind lost in a haze of terror and hypothermia. His lips were blue, his skin unnaturally cold to the touch, and his eyes, when he managed to open them, held only a vacant, frozen fear.

The sight of Wesley, barely coherent and bearing the fresh marks of Flint's brutality, ignited a fierce public outcry. The town, already simmering with unease, erupted. Questions were demanded, accusations hurled. The Selectmen, facing a furious populace and the undeniable evidence of Flint's mismanagement and cruelty, knew they had no choice. A swift, emergency meeting was called. The decision was unanimous and unequivocal: Philemon Flint must go! His reign of "efficiency" was abruptly and ignominiously over.

Chapter 11

The disappearance of Wesley, coupled with the grim, unspoken truths whispered about Harriet's death, had left the Overseers of the Poor visibly reeling. Their carefully constructed façade of responsible governance lay shattered, evident in the tight lines around their mouths and the way they avoided each other's eyes. They could no longer ignore the growing discontent that hummed through Pondicherry like a low, angry beehive. A new superintendent was desperately needed, someone capable of mending the town's fractured trust and restoring a semblance of humanity to the Town Farm. Their search, conducted with an urgency that bordered on panic, led them to Obediah Clark and his wife, Constance.

The very air at the Town Farm seemed to soften with Obediah Clark's arrival. The heavy, oppressive silence that had hung like a shroud under Flint's rule was replaced by a quieter, more human rhythm. Obediah was a man built of softer stuff, his shoulders rounded, his eyes large and kind, prone to crinkling at the corners when he listened. He often paused in the keeping room, his hands clasped behind his back, his head cocked, genuinely listening to the inmates' low murmurs of complaint or their halting requests. He'd nod, his brow furrowed with a concern that was palpable, and though he might not always be able to grant their wishes, the mere act of being heard was a visible balm, smoothing away some of the inmates' perpetual tension.

The sharp crack of Flint's whip was gone, replaced by Obediah's gentle, if often ineffective, encouragement. Discipline, when it occurred, was a rare, quiet reprimand delivered in hushed tones, never a brutal spectacle. He felt a genuine sympathy for their plight, his very presence a noticeable, if fragile, shift towards compassion.

For Ned Lakin, confined to his bed under the eaves, Obediah Clark was a bittersweet change. The biting scorn of Flint had vanished, replaced by a gentle solicitude. Obediah often visited the small room, his large, kind eyes filled with pity as he looked at Ned's twisted leg. "Poor boy, poor, poor boy," he'd murmur, sometimes patting Ned's hand with a soft, warm touch. He'd sit on the edge of the cot for a few moments, listening patiently as Ned, emboldened by the kindness, occasionally spoke of his dreams for books, or the faint hope that one day his leg might mend. Obediah would nod, his brow furrowed with genuine sorrow, and assure Ned that God was kind and perhaps a new book would come his way. But no new books ever materialized, nor any practical suggestion for his mending leg. The pity was a comfort, a welcome warmth after Flint's cold disdain, but it was also a stagnant pool, offering no path forward, no tangible hope for a change in his confined existence. Ned would look at his small stack of old, worn books, their stories fading, and feel the dust of unread pages settling on his own spirit.

Yet, as the seasons turned, a different kind of tension began to settle over the Farm—a quiet, gnawing frustration. Obediah's kindness was undeniable, but his head was no match for his heart when it came to the unforgiving demands of farm management. He might admire a healthy stand of corn with a wistful sigh, but he seemed utterly blind to the subtleties of soil quality or the precise timing for planting. Crops, once meager under Flint, now withered more visibly in the fields, their stalks thin, their yields pitiful. A sickly yellow seemed to leach into the green of the summer crops. The dairy cow, under his supervision, developed a persistent, wet cough that Obediah merely patted with a worried frown, and the pigs, despite his kind words, seemed perpetually underfed, their ribs too prominent beneath their bristly hides. Tools, once honed by Edwin under Flint's rigid demands, now lay scattered and rusted in the barn, regularly breaking from neglect or clumsy misuse. The tang of neglect replaced the scent of honest labor. The farm's output plummeted, its meager yields straining town resources despite Obediah's good intentions. The Overseers, poring over increasingly bleak ledgers, began to rub their temples, their initial relief at Flint's departure slowly replaced by a growing, nagging frustration that tightened their lips.

Cyril Cross, a neighboring farmer with hands like gnarled oak and a face weathered by sun and wind, would often ride over to offer advice, seeing the honest struggle reflected in Obediah's earnest eyes. He tried to teach him, patiently explaining the nuances of crop rotation or the subtle signs of ailing livestock, but Obediah's mind simply wasn't built for the intricate dance of the land. His eyes would glaze over, and his responses would be vague nods of agreement that promised nothing.

One blustery afternoon, the ringing clang of steel and the smell of hot metal announced the arrival of Leander Frost, the local blacksmith. Leander was a burly man, his forearms thick with roiling muscle, his face perpetually smudged with the fine dust of his trade. He'd come to shoe the two plow horses, sturdy beasts that also served to pull the wagon into town for supplies—a heavy necessity for any animal tasked with such relentless labor. As he worked, hammering and shaping iron at his portable forge set up in the farmyard, Leander noticed Edwin. The boy moved among the powerful animals with an easy, almost silent grace, his hands confident as he stroked their muzzles, murmuring quiet words that only the horses seemed to hear. Edwin knew each horse's temperament, how to approach the skittish mare with gentle assurance, how to soothe the grumpy gelding with a soft hand on its flank. Leander watched him, genuinely impressed, a spark of recognition in his soot-rimmed eyes. This was more than just farm work; it was a rare, intuitive connection.

Later, wiping sweat from his brow with a grimy rag, Mr. Frost approached Obediah. "That boy, Edwin," he began, a glint in his soot-rimmed eyes, "he's got a true gift with horses. A real touch. I could use an apprentice like him down at the smithy. Teach him the trade proper."

Obediah, always keen to see his residents find a better path, beamed, his face brightening with genuine pleasure. "An excellent idea, Mr. Frost! A fine trade for a capable lad. I'll check with the Overseers straight away!"

For Edwin, Leander Frost's words were more than just an offer; they were a lifeline cast into a dark, swirling sea. The Farm, with its relentless drudgery and stifling confinement, felt like a slow, inexorable burial. He saw no future here, only endless days stretching out like the barren fields, promising nothing but toil and a quiet fade into an unmarked grave like his mother's. But the smithy—the roar of the forge, the rhythmic clang of hammer on anvil, the smell of hot metal and singed hoof—that was a real trade. It was a skill that could take him anywhere, give him an independence he'd only dreamed of. To work with horses, truly work with them, not just harness them for endless plowing. To live in town, to earn a wage, to build something with his own hands that wasn't just torn from the earth by brute force. The idea ignited a desperate, consuming hope within him, a burning desire that pulsed in his veins, urging him to escape the shadow of the Farm and forge a life for himself beyond its desolate confines. He could almost feel the heat of the forge on his face, taste the grit of coal dust, hear the symphony of a real workshop.

The idea was indeed discussed by the Overseers of the Poor. It offered a flicker of hope for Edwin's future, a rare chance to escape the Farm. But the flicker was quickly extinguished. Senator Libby, a powerful figure whose influence stretched far beyond the town lines, summarily vetoed the idea. His reasoning, presented with a cool, unassailable logic, was that Edwin was one of the very few fully able and knowledgeable people on the farm, too valuable to lose. "His labor is indispensable to the Farm's continued operation," Libby stated, his voice flat and final, his gaze unyielding. What Obediah and the Overseers didn't know, however, was Libby's true motive: a tether binding Edwin to this forgotten patch of earth. The Senator had good reason to keep Edwin a nameless pauper. His presence on the Farm served a deeper purpose, protecting secrets buried longer and deeper than Harriet Woodbury herself.

Chapter 12

The air in the Selectmen's meeting room was thick with the scent of pipe tobacco and unspoken frustration. The Selectmen, pillars of Pondicherry society, sat around a polished oak table, their faces grim under the gaslight, the shadows deepening the lines of worry on their brows. Before them sat Obediah Clark, fidgeting ceaselessly with the brim of his hat, his kind eyes clouded with an anxiety that seemed almost physically manifest.

"Mr. Clark," Nat Libby, the head Selectman, began, his voice cool and measured, betraying no outward emotion despite the subtle weariness in his eyes. He leaned forward slightly, tapping a thick ledger with a deliberate finger. "We appreciate your efforts to bring... a gentler hand to the Town Farm. We truly do. The reports from the inmates themselves speak to your compassion." He paused, letting the heavy silence underscore his next words. "However, the ledger itself tells a different story. A grim one, Mr. Clark."

Josiah Croft, another Selectman, leaned forward, his voice sharper, his patience clearly wearing thin. "The records from Flint's time, while... unpalatable in their methods, at least showed some contribution. Sales of livestock, surplus crops. We expected the Farm, if not to turn a profit, then at least to offset its own costs. But look here." He pushed the damning ledger across the table towards Obediah, the heavy book thudding against the wood. "Thomas Albright here compiled these figures. Yields are down by nearly two-thirds this quarter. The east field, which should have seen a second planting, lies fallow, choked with weeds. The livestock numbers... frankly, they're alarming. We're spending more cash on the Farm than ever before, simply to keep its residents fed, clothed, and warmed."

Obediah wrung his hat, his knuckles white. "I've tried, gentlemen. Truly. The soil is stubborn, and the season was hard. And I simply cannot bring myself to... to drive the residents as Mr. Flint did. They are human beings, deserving of dignity." His voice trailed off, a plea in his eyes.

"Dignity doesn't feed them when the harvest fails, Obediah," Josiah Croft countered, his tone hardening, his jaw set. "Pondicherry's coffers aren't limitless. We cannot continue to pour money into a venture that consistently fails to produce."

Nat Libby's gaze swept over the table, encompassing the other Selectmen, a silent acknowledgment passing between them, before settling back on Obediah. "The purpose of the Farm, while providing for the indigent, is also to instill industry. To make them self-sufficient. This current approach, while benevolent, undermines that fundamental principle, and at considerable public expense." The unspoken conclusion hung in the air, a crushing weight: Obediah Clark was not equipped for the job.

Reluctantly, with heavy sighs and strained expressions, the Selectmen reached their decision. Obediah, despite his good heart, would have to go.

That decision, however, was overshadowed by a far more immediate crisis only a week later. A careless tramp, seeking warmth and shelter from the biting cold, had crept into the Town Farm's barn, leaving behind a smoldering cigarette in a pile of hay. By the time the first wisps of smoke curled under the eaves, thin as ghosts against the pre-dawn sky, the fire was already roaring, a hungry beast consuming the dry timber from within. The air filled with the sharp, acrid scent of burning wood and terrified animal. The very ground seemed to vibrate with the escalating roar.

The cries of "Fire!" ripped through the predawn quiet like a physical blow. Inmates stumbled from their beds, some disoriented and bewildered by the sudden light, others galvanized by sheer terror. Flames already licked greedily at the dry timbers of the barn, casting a hellish orange glow across the farmyard that danced on the faces of the terrified onlookers. From inside, the desperate bellows of the animals—Bessie the milk cow, Nell and Charley the draft horses, the pigs—screamed in primal panic, their terrified cries echoing the crackle and roar of the blaze.

Obediah Clark rushed out, his nightshirt flapping, his face pale and contorted with horror. He immediately began shouting directions, a flurry of well-meaning but utterly uncoordinated commands. "Buckets! Get water! Form a line! Hurry, for goodness sake!"

Silas was already moving, grabbing a bucket and scrambling towards the well with surprising agility. Cyril Cross, awakened by the commotion at his nearby farm, was already galloping across the fields on horseback, a grim set to his jaw. He was the first to reach the blazing barn doors, assessing the inferno with a farmer's practiced eye, his breath catching in his throat. "No! Water won't do it yet! We need to get the animals out! The roof's going to go any second!"

But the animals, maddened by the searing heat and choking smoke, were refusing to budge from their stalls, their instincts overwhelmed by terror. Nell and Charley bucked and reared against their halters, their eyes rolling white with fear. Bessie lowed piteously, huddled in a corner, trembling uncontrollably. The smoke was thick, acrid, burning the lungs and stinging the eyes.

Then, through the chaos, Edwin moved. His heart hammered against his ribs, a frantic drumbeat, but a strange, focused calm settled over him. It wasn't bravery, but an instinct, a knowledge of these creatures deeper than fear. He ignored Obediah's frantic instructions, ignored the roaring flames that threatened to consume them all. His gaze was fixed on the terrified, wide eyes of Bessie, the old milk cow, trapped in her stall. He pushed past the flailing, shouting inmates, moving with a quiet purpose, straight into the smoke-filled barn, a wet rag clutched over his mouth and nose. "Come on, girl," he croaked, his voice surprisingly steady despite the burning in his throat, as he reached Bessie's head, stroking her nose, whispering soft, familiar words that she knew from a thousand quiet mornings. He untied her lead, pulling gently but firmly. The cow, usually placid and stubborn, hesitated for a moment, then seemed to recognize his scent, his touch, his quiet authority. She lowed nervously but allowed him to guide her towards the opening. One by one, Edwin moved through the stalls, cutting ropes, murmuring to each terrified animal, his hands steady, his touch conveying a reassurance no shout could. He slapped the flanks of the panicked pigs, urging them forward, his quiet command a stark contrast to the shouting and chaos outside. His touch seemed to momentarily cut through their terror, their instincts overridden by their deep, long-standing trust in the boy who cared for them daily.

Cyril Cross plunged in behind him, a grim shadow in the smoke, directing the freed animals toward the wide-open barn doors and then helping Obediah organize a desperate bucket brigade from the well. Silas worked alongside Edwin, helping to calm the smaller animals and prod them out into the biting morning air. The heat was immense, searing their skin, but Edwin didn't stop until every last hoof and claw was out of the collapsing structure.

They saved every animal, a miraculous feat. But the barn itself was not so lucky. The roof eventually gave way with a thunderous roar, sending a shower of sparks into the night sky like a dying gasp. When the last embers glowed, the barn stood as a charred, skeletal ruin, its southern wall entirely gone, much of its roof collapsed inwards. The animals were safe, huddled outside, breathing heavily, their flanks still radiating heat, eyes wide with the lingering shock of the fire. But the structure, so vital to the farm's operation, had sustained costly, catastrophic damage. The flames had been extinguished, but a new, immense financial burden now loomed over the Town Farm, eclipsing even Obediah's compassionate but inefficient management.

Chapter 13

The smoldering ruins of the Town Farm barn became a physical scar on the landscape of Pondicherry, a stark, blackened monument to inefficiency and neglect. Long after the last ember had died, the acrid scent of charred timber still clung to the air, carried by the biting winds, a constant, pervasive reminder. But the physical damage paled in comparison to the fire it ignited within the town itself. The blaze hadn't merely consumed timbers and hay; its monstrous orange glow, visible for miles in the pre-dawn darkness, had threatened the very farms that bordered the Town Farm. Farmers, roused from their sleep by frantic shouts, had stood by their own barns, axes clutched in hand, their faces pale with the terrifying realization of how easily the inferno could have spread, consuming their livelihoods, their precious livestock, their winter feed. Mothers pulled their children closer, the lingering fear a cold knot in their stomachs.

The grumbling that had simmered beneath the surface about the increasing costs of the Farm under Obediah now boiled over into an open rage. The carelessness, the sheer negligence that allowed a vagrant's ember to nearly level an entire section of Pondicherry, was laid squarely at the feet of the Town Farm's lax oversight. Conversations in the general store, once hushed whispers exchanged over barrels of flour, now turned into furious declarations. Customers slammed coins onto counters, their voices rising, demanding accountability. The air vibrated with their indignation, a tangible hum of collective anger. "My pasture almost caught!" cried one farmer, his fist thudding the counter. "And that barn was paid for with our money, not Clark's!" Every citizen saw the Farm, no longer as a distant charity, but as a direct, public, and very dangerous liability.

Demands for answers, and more importantly, for immediate action, swelled into an irresistible tide. Hands, hardened by years of labor, scrawled furious names onto petitions that circulated from church doors to tavern counters, each signature a decisive stroke of public will. The Selectmen, already grappling with the quiet decision to dismiss Obediah, suddenly found themselves facing a far greater tempest than they had anticipated.

An emergency town meeting was called within days of the fire, and the Town Hall was packed to overflowing. Every bench creaked under the weight of anxious citizens, their bodies pressed together so tightly that the air grew warm and thick with the collective anxiety and indignation of Pondicherry. Citizens spilled into the aisles, their faces grim and expectant, a low, restless hum filling the room, steadily growing in volume. The single gaslight above the podium flickered nervously, casting dancing shadows that mimicked the unrest.

When Nat Libby, the head Selectman, stepped to the podium, a restless murmur rippled through the crowd, quickly swelling to an agitated roar. He raised a hand, attempting to speak, but his voice was drowned out before he could utter a single word.

"What are you going to do about it, Nat?" Old Man Porter, a burly farmer from the back, bellowed, his face flushed, veins throbbing in his neck. "My woodlot almost went up last week! And all the money we put into that barn went up in smoke!"

"The Farm's a drain!" another voice, sharp and high-pitched, cut through the din. "Costs us more than it ever brings in! It's a bottomless pit!"

Josiah Croft, his usual calm demeanor strained, attempted to quiet the room, his pleas lost in a rising tide of shouts and complaints. Thomas Albright, pale and agitated, kept glancing nervously at the swinging doors, as if expecting further chaos to burst through them. Nat Libby pounded his gavel repeatedly, the sharp crack swallowed by the sustained clamor, a futile sound against the wave of public fury. Even he, usually so composed and unreadable, shifted uncomfortably in his seat, his cool demeanor visibly tested by the sheer volume of public wrath. For the first time in memory, a bead of sweat traced a path down his temple.

The message was clear, delivered with an urgency that brooked no argument. "You either get that Town Farm under control!" one woman, her voice surprisingly strong and clear, pierced through the din, her eyes blazing, "or you shut it down altogether!" Her words were met with a thunderous roar of agreement, a stomping of feet, and a scraping of benches as the entire assembly rose to its feet in a unified, angry demand.

Nat Libby finally managed to force his voice above the din, his tone firm, cutting through the anger with a practiced authority that demanded attention. "Order! Order, please! The Selectmen hear your concerns! Let it be known, a search for a new superintendent, one who can restore both order and productivity to the Farm, will begin immediately! We will not rest until this situation is resolved to the satisfaction and safety of all Pondicherry residents!"

A tense quiet settled over the hall as the townfolk, though still simmering, began to slowly disperse, their faces still set but their immediate fury somewhat assuaged. The Selectmen exchanged uneasy, exhausted glances, the weight of the moment pressing down on them. The stakes had just been raised, pushed by the furious citizens to an uncomfortable height. The Town Farm, once a quiet, unavoidable expense, was now a public powder keg, a single spark away from complete conflagration, and they, the Selectmen, were standing squarely on top of it. They had to act decisively, not just for the town's strained finances, but for its very peace. A new superintendent, far more capable and perhaps less compassionate than Obediah, was not just desirable, but absolutely essential. And the future of the Farm itself, once seemingly assured, was now on the precipice of closure.

Chapter 14

The clamor of the emergency town meeting still echoed in the ears of the Pondicherry Selectmen, a stark reminder of the ultimatum they now faced. The memory of Flint's casual brutality was a sour taste, but Obediah's heartfelt inefficiency had proved equally disastrous, underscored by the charred remains of the barn. Their new superintendent could not be another tyrant, nor another well-meaning failure. They needed competence, above all else – a steady hand, a sharp mind for figures, and a firm will. Someone who understood farming, managed finances, and wouldn't ignite public outrage or literal fires. The ideal candidate, they agreed, would be a man of practical mind, firm but fair, capable of restoring both the Farm's output and its good name.

Their search led them to Franklin "Frank" Haines. On paper, Haines was precisely what Pondicherry needed. His application boasted a decade of successful farming, with reports of healthy harvests and well-maintained livestock from his previous town. His references spoke of a steady hand and a keen eye for efficiency, painting a picture of quiet authority and practical knowledge. To the Selectmen, particularly Nat Libby, he represented the perfect middle ground: a man who projected an air of competence, promising a return to stability and, crucially, a reduction in public expenditure. They did not know that Haines's success had largely been due to an exceptionally diligent foreman, now deceased, whose quiet competence had masked his employer's profound apathy. Haines, for his part, saw the Superintendent's job not as a mission, but as a welcome haven – a steady salary, a secure roof over his head, and the enticing prospect of minimal effort. His wife,

Ruth, who would serve as Matron, seemed equally inclined towards a quiet, undemanding life.

Frank and Ruth Haines arrived in Pondicherry to the immediate, daunting task of the burned barn. Its skeletal remains stood stark against the winter sky, a constant, blackened reminder of the Farm's troubles. The animals, saved by Edwin, Silas, Obediah, and Cyril Cross, were housed in makeshift shelters, shivering against the cold wind that whistled through the makeshift walls. The need for reconstruction was urgent, expensive, and a clear test of the new superintendent's mettle. Haines, however, tackled the challenge with a detached air. He oversaw the initial clearing of debris and the eventual construction with a nominal presence, his hands often clasped behind his back as he surveyed the work from a slight distance. The complex task of identifying and acquiring suitable materials, the meticulous carpentry, and the practical planning of new animal housing quickly fell to the few able-bodied inmates, primarily Edwin, and especially to Cyril Cross, whose generous advice and direct involvement proved invaluable. Haines would occasionally stroll through the reconstruction site, offering a curt nod or a vague, unhelpful instruction ("Looks like you need more wood there," he might say, without specifying type or quantity), before retreating to the warmth of the farmhouse. The scent of damp, unburnt wood seemed to cling to him, not the rich, earthy smell of actual labor.

Upstairs, in the room under the eaves, Ned Lakin became almost invisible under Frank Haines. Haines rarely, if ever, ventured into the third-floor room. If he thought of Ned at all, it was likely as a permanent, immovable fixture, requiring no more attention than the bed he occupied. The small stack of well-worn books by Ned's cot remained untouched, no new volumes appearing to replace those he had long since memorized. Requests for fresh reading material, if Edwin or Wesley dared to voice them, met with a blank stare, as if the very idea was unfathomable. Ned lay in his bed, listening to the muffled sounds of the farm below, the distant thud of hammers on new timbers, the shouts of the working men. He yearned for the adventure of his books, for the escape they offered, but in the quiet, dusty solitude of his room, the world beyond his window began to feel smaller, the promise of new tales dwindling to a whisper. The air in his room, once thick with imagined forests and rolling seas, now tasted only of dust and stagnation.

It was during this period of rebuilding that a new, unexpected presence arrived at the Farm. Jonathan Moss appeared one crisp morning, emerging from the mist like a figure from a forgotten tale. He was a man in his mid-forties. His clothes, though patched and worn, were meticulously clean, speaking more of honest wear than neglect. His beard was neatly trimmed, and his eyes, though framed by sun-creased wrinkles, were remarkably bright and filled with an almost childlike curiosity, missing nothing. He carried a worn leather satchel, seemingly innocuous, but hinting at more than just a vagabond's meager possessions. He sought shelter not out of destitution, but out of convenience, a need for temporary rest, and perhaps a quiet curiosity about the microcosm of human life found within the Farm's walls. He immediately offered his help with the daunting task of clearing the fire debris, approaching the arduous work with a quiet diligence that set him apart. He particularly enjoyed sawing and splitting wood, finding a meditative rhythm in the swing of the axe and the satisfying thud of timber breaking apart. He hummed a low, tuneless melody to himself. Occasionally, he'd pause to offer a profound, yet simply phrased, observation about the strength of the wood grain, the biting crispness of the winter air, or the inexorable passage of time. He moved with an almost imperceptible lightness, as if his feet barely touched the hard earth.

Haines's true management style soon settled into a predictable rhythm. Frank Haines was not actively cruel, but he was profoundly apathetic. His days were spent by the hearth, poring over old newspapers, his spectacles perched on his nose, or indulging in long, undisturbed naps in a worn armchair, often rousing only to call for another cup of tea. Matron Ruth, equally disinclined to exert herself, largely managed the kitchen and basic care, often leaning heavily on Bethiah, a long-suffering servant woman whose quiet efficiency kept the household running. The demanding work of the farm – the mending of fences, the tending of fields, the feeding of animals – was unofficially but firmly pushed onto the most capable residents, Edwin chief among them. Jonathan Moss's willing efforts during the barn reconstruction only served to further enable Haines's indolence, providing another pair of hands that required no direct supervision.

For Edwin, however, Jonathan became a breath of fresh air, a window to a world beyond the farm's confining fences. Jonathan would spend hours talking to the boy during breaks, sometimes leaning against a half-finished barn wall as the winter winds bit, sometimes beside the steaming troughs where Edwin fed the animals, the warmth of the hay rising around them. He spoke of the vast, untamed wilderness of Maine—of remote streams where brook trout flashed silver, their scales catching the sun, of hidden clearings deep in the woods where ancient pines touched the sky like sentinels, of mountains that rose like sleeping giants, their peaks dusted with snow.

"See that sparrow, Edwin?" Jonathan once pointed, his finger tracing the quick, erratic flight of a common brown bird. "Most folks just see a brown blur. But listen. Hear how his call changes when a hawk circles high above? He's a tiny guard, warning the whole forest." He showed Edwin how to read the damp earth by the creek, distinguishing a raccoon's splayed, hand-like paw prints from a fox's delicate, almost perfectly aligned tracks. "Every creature leaves a story, if you know how to read the language of their travels." He'd talk about the fierce resilience of a fiddlehead fern pushing through cold soil in the spring, or the way a jack pine grew twisted and strong against the wind blowing across Bald Pate, its roots clinging stubbornly to the rocky ground.

With his words, he painted pictures of the sea: the vast, shimmering expanse of the ocean, stretching blue to meet the sky, the thunderous crash of waves against jagged, granite cliffs, the sharp, invigorating tang of salt and brine carried on the wind, and the lonely, haunting cry of gulls circling overhead. He spoke of islands shrouded in mist, of distant lighthouses blinking like solitary eyes in the fog, and the immense, untamed power that made even the mightiest trees bow.

Sometimes, he would even produce a worn journal from his satchel, filled with intricate, yet precise, sketches of birds in flight, different leaves rendered with meticulous detail, or the stark, elegant lines of animal tracks on a muddy bank. "This is true wealth, boy," he'd whisper, his eyes alight with a deep, quiet passion. "To know the land, to understand its rhythms. It asks nothing of you but observation, and it gives everything." Edwin, who had known only the grim realities of the farm, was utterly mesmerized by Jonathan's gentle spirit and his optimistic, almost poetic, view of life. He admired Jonathan's intellectual freedom, his quiet dignity, and the sheer audacity of living life on one's own terms, even if it meant appearing as a simple "tramp."

This newfound perspective, this intoxicating glimpse of a life unbound, stirred a powerful yearning within Edwin, a deep, restless ache that the farm's routines could no longer dull. One hesitant morning, catching Haines alone in the kitchen, half-hidden behind the morning paper, Edwin found the courage to speak. His hands clenched slightly behind his back, his voice a little tight with suppressed hope. "Mr. Haines, sir," he began. "Mr. Frost, the blacksmith, he... he offered me an apprenticeship. Would you... would you consider letting me go? I could learn a trade, support myself."

Haines barely looked up from his newspaper, its pages rustling faintly. A faint sigh escaped him, an almost imperceptible ripple of irritation crossing his face. "An apprenticeship? Nonsense, boy. You're far too valuable here. We've just rebuilt the barn; the horses need tending, the fields. You're one of the only ones truly capable." He waved a dismissive hand, the gesture final, his gaze returning to the printed page. "No need to trouble the Overseers with such a foolish notion. Your place is here." The words, delivered with such casual indifference, landed like a heavy blow. Edwin felt a cold knot form in his stomach, spreading through his chest, extinguishing the warmth Jonathan's stories had ignited. He stood there for a long moment, numb, the glimmer of hope flickering and dying, leaving behind only the bitter taste of ash.

A few weeks later, as quietly and unceremoniously as he had arrived, Jonathan Moss moved on. He simply packed his worn satchel one dawn, gave a brief, knowing smile to Edwin that held both farewell and encouragement, and then vanished down the road, swallowed by the rising mist as if he were merely a part of the landscape returning to itself. The silence he left behind felt vast, a gaping hole in Edwin's days. The vibrant stories, the shared observations of hidden life, the whispered dreams of freedom—all gone. A heavy cloak of despair settled over Edwin, pressing down on his chest. Was this truly his lot in life? To be forever confined to these fields, tending other men's animals, living under other men's whims? To never have a life of his own choosing, to never forge his own path beyond the dreary confines of the Pondicherry Town Farm? The question gnawed at him, relentless and bitter, a constant, sharp ache.

Under Haines, the Town Farm limped along. It never thrived, never quite spiraled into catastrophic failure, but it certainly never improved. Rations were adequate, but never generous, precisely enough to sustain the body but not the spirit. Maintenance was deferred until absolutely necessary; leaking roofs dripped into buckets for weeks before a patch was reluctantly applied, broken tools lay rusting in corners until their absence became critical, forcing a grudging repair. Infrastructure slowly decayed, but quietly, incrementally, like an ignored tooth. The residents of the Town Farm learned a new kind of survival: if they stayed quiet, did their minimal work without complaint, and avoided drawing attention, they would mostly be left alone, navigating their stagnant existence in the shadow of their indifferent keeper. But for Edwin, Jonathan's presence had ignited a new, dangerous spark – a vision of a world where one could be truly free, truly self-possessed, even without land or title. The contrast between the Farm's dull reality and Jonathan's vibrant philosophy would continue to gnaw at him, a constant, sharp ache.

Chapter 15

The biting winter winds that swept across Pondicherry often carried more than just snow and cold; sometimes, they brought news—news that could chill a body more deeply than any frost. Such was the case with the story that began to trickle from the neighboring town of Denmark, a tale that spread through the farm communities like wildfire, igniting fear and unease.

Superintendent Frank Haines, settled deeply into his armchair by the hearth, barely glanced up from his newspaper when his wife, Ruth, gasped. She held the *Pondicherry Chronicle* with trembling hands, its front page screaming a headline that pierced the comfortable quiet he so valued:

"SENSATION OF THE HOUR! MURDEROUS ASSAULT ON DENMARK MA-TRON!"

The article detailed a brutal attack: *"The sensation of the hour is the murderous assault made, Saturday morning, by a tramp upon the wife of Superintendent Elbridge Thorn of Denmark poor farm. The tramp whose name we fail to learn, is a middle-aged, thick-set, powerful man, of nearly 200 pounds weight, and well known to Mr. Thorn and other town farm superintendents thereabout, he going repeatedly from one town farm to another and making a stay of days or even weeks, and daily doing a great amount of hard labor, especially at working up big wood piles, in return for which he asks only his board and tobacco. So far as is known, the present instance is the only one of the kind to indicate that he is anything but a quiet, well-behaved harmless person. Friday evening, in the kindness of her heart, Mrs. Thorn gave the man a pair of mittens. Next morning he came downstairs, and finding his benefactress alone in the room, he flung the mittens at her, with an oath, and then passed out, muttering something to the effect that he'd 'settle with her later!' He immediately returned with a seven-pound hardwood billet in his hands, and suddenly advanced upon the terrified woman, aiming a deadly blow at her head. This, she dodged sufficiently to escape its full force, but the billet grazing her head, felled her to the floor, rendering her unconscious. Her screams as the tramp attacked her were heard by her husband in the barn, adjoining, who rushed to the rescue, the assailant darting out another door as he came in after seeing that his wife was cared for, Mr. Thorn, with loaded musket, started out to overhaul the man, but he was nowhere to be seen, and made good his escape to parts unknown. Mrs. Thorn was not seriously injured, but there is little doubt but that she would have been instantly killed had she received the full force of the titanic blow. It is believed that the man is insane."*

Ruth's face was ashen, her eyes wide with unadulterated fear. "Frank," she whispered, her voice thin. "Did you read this? A tramp... he attacked the matron! With a club!"

Haines merely grunted, lowering his paper just enough to peer over the top. "Hmph. Denmark. Always trouble in Denmark." He knew the type—the itinerants who wandered the poor farm circuit. He recognized the description. "Sounds like Blabon. Albert Blabon. Comes through here sometimes for wood-chopping. Quiet fellow, usually." He offered this last observation with a shrug, then raised his newspaper again, dismissing the incident as distant news, not his problem. The inconvenience of her rising anxiety was more irritating to him than the details of the assault itself.

But for Ruth, the confirmation that the attacker was a known figure, a man who had walked their very halls, sent a jolt of icy dread through her. Albert Blabon. She had given that man extra rations, a warm blanket. And he was still at large.

For the next several days, a cold apprehension clung to Ruth like a shroud. Every shadow seemed to hold a lurking figure, every creak of the old farm-house sent a jolt of fear through her. Her breath often hitched in her throat, a tight knot forming in her stomach. She found herself watching the inmates more closely, her gaze lingering on the quiet ones, the powerful ones, the ones Frank dismissed as harmless. The "kindness of her heart" that Mrs. Thorn had shown, giving mittens, now seemed like a dangerous vulnerability. She kept the doors locked, even during the day, and eyed the woods bordering the farm with suspicion.

Then, a week later, another headline from the *Pondicherry Chronicle* brought both a measure of relief and a fresh wave of terror:

"ASSAILANT APPREHENDED!"

The article stated: *"On Mar 3d, Albert Blabon, hailing from Chesterville, was arraigned before the Supreme Judicial Court at Paris for assault with a club upon Mrs. Mehitable Thorn, wife of Elbridge Thorn, superintendent of our poor farm, he having been indicted in February on this court. He pleaded not guilty, and his trial was set for Mar 12th."*

He was caught. A wave of shaky relief washed over Ruth, but it was quickly swamped by a new fear that deepened into a paranoia. That same week, the newspaper carried another chilling report, this time from Exeter:

"MADMAN ESCAPES EXETER POOR FARM!"

The brief report continued: *"A madman at Exeter poor farm escaped from his cage, burned the buildings, and killed a woman against whom he had a crazy grudge."*

And another terrible tale from Otisfield, not far away from Pondicherry:

An East Otisfield man has written to a Lewiston Police Matron asking her to give him a good boy about eight or ten years of age for adoption after probation. This gentleman, who is a farmer, has had hard luck with boys. Not long ago he came to Lewiston and took a boy from the Lewiston poor farm, and carried him home, after buying him a new suit of clothes, toys and playthings. The next day after the boy got there twenty of the farm hens were found killed. They had been murdered in a fiendish way, each head being crushed by the heel of a boot. The next day all the ducks on the farm were killed the same way, and the next, the last of the poultry turned up its toes in the same mysterious way. It was a day or two after this while passing through a shed the farmer found a trap of an ingenious fashion. It consisted of a sharp axe fixed in position where the baby of the farm was in the habit of playing, with the evident intention that the child should fall over it and be killed. The next train brought the boy back to Lewiston, and the poor farm at South Lewiston is his happy owner now.

The image of a "madman" escaping a "cage" and committing murder burrowed into Ruth's mind, feeding a burgeoning terror. Albert Blabon was apprehended, yes, but what about the next one? That Lewiston boy? How terrifying! The news confirmed what her deepest fears now whispered: the poor farms were breeding grounds for madness, and their residents, the very people they were supposed to care for, were unpredictable, capable of terrifying violence.

Ruth began to see a madman around every corner. Every quiet resident seemed to harbor a hidden rage, every glance held a potential threat. Her usual disinterest in the inmates curdled into a pervasive, self-protective fear. The idea of staying another year, living side-by-side with these people, became increasingly unbearable. Her sleep became fitful, haunted by imagined screams and the rustle of unseen intruders.

A few weeks later, the *Pondicherry Chronicle* delivered the final chilling detail of the Denmark assault. Ruth, though she tried to avoid the news from other poor farms, found her eyes drawn to the stark black print, unable to look away from the unfolding horror.

"BLABON GUILTY OF ASSAULT ON DENMARK MATRON!"

The paper concluded: *"At the trial of Albert Blabon, on the charge of assault upon Mrs. Elbridge Thorn, matron of Denmark poor farm, three witnesses testified how he attacked her with a club Dec. 8th, inflicting injuries which nearly caused her death, and his only provocation was that she had, out of kindness, given him a pair of mittens on a cold day. Blabon made a general denial. He, however, was adjudged guilty and was sentenced to ten months in the county jail. The testimony of the witnesses fully accords with the report published in the "Chronicle" at the time."*

Ruth read the verdict, the details of the attack laid bare once more. "*Nearly caused her death*," the paper stated, for an act of kindness. The sheer, irrational violence of it settled deep within her. Ten months in jail. Then what? The knowledge that Blabon, a man they knew, could turn so violently with so little provocation, and that he would eventually be released, solidified her resolve. She looked at Frank, her face pale but determined. Their time at the Pondicherry Town Farm, already a struggle, now felt truly perilous.

The fear that had taken root in Ruth's heart blossomed into full-blown terror in the weeks that followed. It gnawed at her, reshaping her every interaction. The residents, once just part of the background, now seemed to carry a latent threat. Even the most familiar faces, seen through the lens of her growing paranoia, seemed capable of sudden, unprovoked violence.

One evening, the small dining room, usually filled with the low drone of conversation and the clatter of spoons, suddenly went silent. The inmates were finishing their meager supper, a thin gruel that hardly filled the stomach. Wesley sat at the end of a long wooden table. Seemingly calm tonight, however, frustration simmered beneath his placid surface. The taste of the bland gruel seemed to scratch at the back of his throat, mirroring the gnawing emptiness in his belly and the unaddressed fear still lingering from Flint's abuse. He picked at his bowl with his spoon, then suddenly, with a sharp, guttural sound of disgust, he pushed the bowl away. It slid across the table, scraping loudly against the rough wood before clattering to the floor, where it spun briefly before settling, empty. It was a small act of protest, a mere burst of exasperation at the bland, unsatisfying meal.

But to Ruth, standing by the kitchen door, clutching a platter of turnips, the sound was an explosion. Her head snapped toward Wesley. She didn't see a weary, hungry man; she saw the "powerful man" from Denmark, the "madman" from Exeter. The murderous child from Lewiston. She saw rage, unreasoning and immediate, behind his tired eyes. The bowl on the floor became a club, the sound of its scrape a prelude to attack.

A high-pitched, choked scream tore from her throat. The platter slipped from her grasp, crashing to the floor, the turnips flying to every corner. Her eyes wide, fixed on Wesley, she stumbled backward, her hand flying to her mouth, shaking violently. "No! Get away!" she gasped, her voice raw, shrinking against the doorframe as if Wesley were about to lunge.

Wesley, startled by her shriek, froze, his own frustration replaced by confusion. He looked from the fallen bowl to Ruth, his brow furrowed, utterly bewildered by her sudden, extreme terror. The other inmates turned, their faces a mixture of surprise and unease.

Frank Haines, who had been sitting at the head of the table, slowly rose, a sigh escaping his lips. His expression held a flicker of annoyance, perhaps even mild disgust. He walked over to Ruth, not with comforting haste, but with a deliberate, weary pace. He didn't put an arm around her, but merely gave a terse instruction. "Ruth, compose yourself. It's just Wesley. He's only upset about his supper." He glanced at Wesley, then back at his trembling wife, his jaw tightening. This was exactly the kind of unpleasantness he had hoped to avoid by taking this position. Her hysterics threatened his quiet, undemanding life. He wanted nothing more than to retreat behind the rustling pages of his newspaper, undisturbed.

The sight of Ruth's uncontrollable fear, her face contorted with unreasoning terror, brought a clear, cold decision to Frank's mind. This job was supposed to be easy. A quiet place, minimal effort. But if Ruth couldn't even manage a dinner table without screaming, their life here would be anything but peaceful. Her anxieties, her breakdowns—they would bring constant trouble and draw unwanted attention to him. He couldn't abide it. He knew then, with an absolute certainty that outweighed any obligation, that they could not, would not, endure another year here. The cost to his own peace and quiet was simply too great. Come April, when their contract was due for renewal, they would leave the Pondicherry Town Farm.

Chapter 16

Under Frank Haines's superintendency, the Pondicherry Town Farm settled into a bleak rhythm of quiet decay. His days, spent primarily by the hearth with a newspaper or indulging in long, undisturbed naps, reflected his profound apathy. As long as the basic functions of the Farm proceeded with minimal effort on his part, he remained detached, oblivious to the subtle but pervasive decline around him. His wife, Ruth, the Matron, mirrored his disinterest, content to manage the household with an equally light hand, relying heavily on the long-suffering Bethiah and the few capable inmates like Edwin.

One blustery afternoon, the unexpected jingle of harness bells announced a rare visitor to the Town Farm. Colonel John Putnam Perley, a pillar of the Pondicherry community and the grandson of Squire Enoch Perley, one of the town's founding fathers, stepped down from his polished carriage. Colonel Perley was a man whose very presence commanded quiet respect, not through bluster, but through a genuine warmth that radiated from him. He was, as some affectionately described him, "that great pumpkin of a man," with a hearty laugh that could fill any room. He had come, as he often did, to visit Mr. and Mrs. Jakes.

Colonel Perley joined the inmates at the dinner table that day, his presence a quiet, dignified disruption to the usual somber meal. As he sat, his gaze fell upon Mr. Jakes, and a gentle smile touched his lips. "Mr. Jakes," he began, his voice carrying clearly across the table, "I was just speaking with young Thomas down at the mill, and it put me in mind of the stories my own father, John, used to tell. He always spoke so highly of working alongside you in those early days, before the consumption took him. Said you had the steadiest hand with a timber he ever saw."

Mr. Jakes, his eyes dim with age, managed a faint, acknowledging nod. Colonel Perley then turned to Mrs. Jakes, his gaze softening further. "And Mrs. Jakes, my Clarissa was just admiring a quilt your ancestors, the Emersons, gifted her family. It's truly remarkable. She often reminds me that her own folk, like your Billy Emerson, worked shoulder-to-shoulder with my grandfather, Squire Enoch, clearing the very ground for his first cabin. A true partnership, right from the start."

Edwin, who usually kept to himself, sat a few seats down, listening, utterly fascinated. He had lived his life on the fringes, without family history or roots. These stories of founding fathers, of generations linked by shared labor and friendship, were like glimpses into a world he'd only imagined. He pictured the land before the town, the arduous work, the enduring bonds that even now, stretched across time to this very table. A faint ache, both of longing and admiration, stirred in his chest.

The conversation, carried mostly by the Colonel, painted a vivid picture for anyone listening. The Jakes were not merely inmates; they were threads in the rich tapestry of Pondicherry's history. Their families' friendship stretched back generations, a bond forged in the town's pioneering spirit. Before Mrs. Jakes's debilitating strokes and Mr. Jakes's slow surrender to the infirmities of old age had brought them to the Farm, they had been a vibrant, contributing part of the community. Colonel Perley and his wife, Clarissa, a benevolent couple deeply involved with the Pondicherry Village Church, made it a point to never forget them. Clarissa frequently sent generous parcels of extra garden truck or supplies, their gifts a testament to their compassionate hearts, often received with a grunt of vague acknowledgment from Frank Haines. Colonel Perley's visit was a brief, precious moment of connection, a glimpse of the vibrant community life the Jakes had once known, before the grey walls of the Town Farm became their world.

◆

The ringing of the school bell, sharp and insistent, was a daily summons Edwin both welcomed and dreaded. Welcomed, because it meant a few hours away from the constant, back-breaking labor of the Farm. Dreaded, because even there, at the Pondicherry one-room schoolhouse, the divisions of his life were stark. He was the only scholar from the Town Farm now, a quiet contrast to the cleaner, brighter children of farmers, merchants, and tradesmen who filled the other desks. The whispers, the averted eyes, the way some mothers pulled their children closer if he ventured too near—Edwin felt it all, a constant, dull ache of stigma.

During noon recess, the schoolyard erupted with shouts and laughter. Edwin usually kept to himself, kicking at loose stones near the woodshed or watching the distant fields, but today, a new presence offered a slight reprieve: Thomas Hale, a lanky boy with intelligent eyes and patched trousers not much better than Edwin's own, from one of the poorer farms on the outskirts of town. Thomas understood the sting of being an outsider. They often shared their meager lunches, comparing stories of farm work.

Today, however, the uneasy peace shattered. Billy Perkins, a bully from the gristmill family just down the road from the Town Farm, a boy whose clothes were worn and mended but still slightly better than the Farm inmates', and whose sneer was always too ready, had cornered Charlie, a timid boy from a struggling farm family, by the outhouse. Billy's family teetered close to the edge themselves, and the fear of slipping into the Town Farm's destitution clung to him like a second skin, making him lash out all the more fiercely at those closest to the brink.

"Look at the charity case," Billy sneered, pushing Charlie's shoulder. "Smells like a pauper, doesn't he?"

Charlie whimpered, his face crumpling. Edwin's blood ran cold. He knew that helpless look. He glanced at Thomas, whose jaw was already tight.

"Leave him be, Perkins!" Edwin called out, his voice sharper than he intended.

Billy turned, his eyes narrowing. "Well, well, if it isn't the mighty Edwin. Come to defend your little mud-caked friends?" He took a step towards Edwin, his cronies snickering behind him. "You ain't nothing but a charity case yourself, Edwin. A bastard. Remember that. A Town Farm nobody."

The words, familiar and yet always stinging, pushed Edwin past his limit. He felt a hot surge of fury. "You leave him alone!" he growled, lunging forward. The contempt in Billy's voice ignited something Edwin had been trying to suppress—the deep, quiet rage at his own helplessness.

Thomas was right beside him. The schoolyard erupted. Fists flew, a blur of coarse wool and dirty knuckles. Billy's sneer vanished, replaced by a surprised grunt as Edwin's fist connected with his jaw. Billy's cronies piled in, and for a few chaotic seconds, it was a tangle of flailing limbs and grunts in the dust.

Then, a booming voice cut through the din. "**BOYS!**"

Master Ingalls, his thin frame surprisingly formidable, plunged into the fray, pulling boys apart with surprising strength. He grabbed Edwin and Billy by their collars, yanking them clear. Their eyes, still blazing, locked across his stern figure.

"What is the meaning of this?!" Master Ingalls demanded, his face red with indignation. The younger children stared, wide-eyed, from a safe distance. The older ones whispered, electrified.

Edwin stood panting, a cut lip throbbing, but a strange, fierce pride swelling in his chest. He'd stood up for Charlie. Thomas, standing a little behind him, gave a barely perceptible nod of shared defiance. Though he knew Master Ingalls's lecture would be long and the consequences unwelcome, for a moment, out there in the dusty schoolyard, Edwin hadn't been a "Town Farm nobody." He'd been Edwin Littlefield, defending his own.

But a far more dangerous threat than schoolyard bullies was already at work in the village. The whisper of scarlet fever had begun its insidious spread through Pondicherry. The epidemic's first victim in the crowded schoolhouses quickly drew the attention of Dr. Bartlett, the town physician. His urgent recommendation was immediately brought before the school board. Reverend William Hague, serving as the school board superintendent, acted swiftly. With no hesitation, he ordered the school dismissed early, sending the children spilling out into the crisp air with an initial whoop of excited, unexpected release, oblivious to the contagion they carried. The epidemic quickly fanned out, sickening one household after another across the community.

At the Town Farm, it began subtly, with a cough that lingered in the keeping room. Then Jane Small, a frail inmate who spent her days knitting by the window, developed a feverish flush on her cheek. It was initially dismissed as a common cold, but soon followed by the tell-tale rash, a fiery red map spreading across her skin. Her throat swelled, and a harsh, dry cough wracked her thin frame. The very air in the farmhouse seemed to thicken, carrying the metallic tang of illness.

Ruth, roused from her usual torpor by the fear of contagion, initially reacted with annoyance. "Just a common fever," she grumbled, waving a dismissive hand. "Keep her away from the others." She left the care to Bethiah, instructing her to bring Jane bowls of lukewarm broth and keep her isolated in her bed. Ruth's hands, usually still, now moved with a brisk, almost frantic energy as she scrubbed surfaces, though she never ventured near the sickroom.

But the fever was not "common." Within days, Mr. Jakes complained of a searing pain in his throat, followed by an angry rash. Then Mrs. Jakes began to sicken, her breathing growing ragged. The Farm, already suffering from neglect, was ill-equipped to handle a full-blown epidemic. There were no isolation wards, no proper medical supplies beyond a few basic salves and tonics.

Frank Haines, when informed of the growing contagion, merely shrugged. "It's the season for such things," he mumbled, refusing to leave his armchair. "Keep them separated. That's all we can do." He delegated all responsibility, leaving Bethiah to navigate the terror of contagion alone, tending to the sick, changing fevered linens, and desperately trying to keep the disease from spreading further into the already vulnerable population. Edwin, with his quiet resilience, assisted where he could, fetching water and helping move the fevered. He found a strange, grim purpose in the midst of the suffering, a stark contrast to the endless, meaningless toil he usually endured.

The dreaded peak came quickly. One cold morning, a week after Mr. Jakes fell ill, his labored breathing stopped. He died quietly in his bed, his face flushed with the fever, his last breath a rattling sigh. His death was a grim, undeniable marker of the epidemic's grip, a stark reminder of the fragile line between life and death in the isolated world of the Town Farm. Mrs. Jakes and Jane Small clung to life, their fevers raging for days, their recovery slow and uncertain. The Farm became a place of hushed coughs and wary glances, a pervasive fear of contagion settling over everyone.

Ruth, already a woman of little sympathy, now viewed the sick with a potent mix of fear and disgust. She retreated further into the farmhouse, disinfecting surfaces with copious amounts of vinegar, and avoiding all direct contact with the inmates, leaving the daily care to Bethiah. The epidemic amplified her existing detachment into a chilling paranoia.

Chapter 17

The departure of Frank Haines, quiet and unceremonious as it was, brought a palpable shift to the Pondicherry Town Farm. His apathy had left a vacuum, a lingering air of neglect that seemed to cling to the very walls. But the town, weary of its poor farm being a constant source of scandal or quiet shame, had acted decisively. Their search led them to Haskell P. Kneeland, a man whose reputation preceded him from his successful management of town farms in neighboring communities.

Kneeland arrived not with a flurry of promises, but with a quiet, observant intensity. He was a man of medium stature, with shrewd, kind eyes that missed nothing and a brisk, purposeful stride. He surveyed the disarray, the worn tools, the listless inmates, and the half-hearted attempts at cultivation with a practiced eye. There was no grand pronouncement, just a steady, methodical application of his philosophy: a town farm, at its core, should be a place of decency, productivity, and, whenever possible, rehabilitation.

Mrs. Kneeland brought her own level of quiet, formidable competence. Her gaze, sharp and assessing, immediately fell upon the inmates' threadbare, ill-fitting clothes. With a soft "Tsk," a sound that spoke volumes of disapproval and efficiency, she quickly took stock of the pitiful state of their garments. Without a word of complaint, she set to work, organizing the mending baskets, sending requests to the town for donations of sturdy fabric and thread, and even, on occasion, sitting herself at a sewing machine to lead the effort to properly clothe every man, woman, and child on the Farm.

But her efforts didn't stop at clothing. The bedding, she soon discovered, was in an even sorrier state – stained, ragged, and offering little comfort against the cold nights. With the same quiet determination, Mrs. Kneeland put out a call to the Pondicherry Village Church ladies, inviting them to a quilting bee right there in the Farm's keeping room.

A week later, the keeping room, usually a place of somber quiet, buzzed with an unfamiliar energy. Piles of collected fabric scraps, vibrant and varied, lay sorted on tables, and the rhythmic snip of scissors mingled with the low hum of chattering voices. A dozen women, many from the church choir and including Mrs. Lewis, sat bent over a large quilting frame, their needles flashing in the lamplight. They sang hymns as they worked, their harmonies adding a spirit of joy to the often bleak confines of the Town Farm. They were creating new bedding, thick and warm, pieced together from remnants that, in their new form, promised comfort and dignity.

Edwin, sent in to fetch a bucket of water, tried to make himself as inconspicuous as possible. He moved quickly, his head down, but it was no use.

"My, my, Edwin Littlefield," a warm voice observed. It was Mrs. Lewis, looking up from a vibrant star-patterned square. Her smile was kind, and her eyes held that familiar, knowing glint. "You seem to grow another inch every time I see you. Why, you're becoming quite the strapping young man."

Edwin felt his cheeks flush, a deep, immediate blush creeping up his neck. He mumbled something unintelligible, clutching the water bucket like a shield. He felt every inch of his lanky, awkward frame under their collective gaze, suddenly acutely aware of his too-short trousers and the rough texture of his skin.

Just then, Mr. Kneeland strolled through the room, a wide smile on his face as he surveyed the industrious scene. "Well now, Mrs. Kneeland," he quipped good-naturedly, "looks like you've got yourself quite the hen party in here! All this clucking and quilting will make this old farm feel like a home again." He winked at the women, who laughed, and then his gaze settled on Edwin, still awkwardly holding the bucket. Kneeland's smile softened. "Good work, Edwin. Keep at it."

Edwin managed a quick, embarrassed nod, avoiding Mrs. Lewis's eyes, and hurried out, the sound of their gentle murmurs and renewed chattering following him. Outside, in the cool evening air, he leaned against the barn door, his face still hot. He might be a "big, strapping young man," but he still felt like a gangly boy, especially under the kind, discerning eyes of Mrs. Lewis.

Under Kneeland's firm yet fair hand, the Farm began to breathe again. Fields that had lain fallow were systematically tilled and planted with a newfound vigor, yielding abundant harvests. The barn, once perpetually in disrepair, saw its roof patched and stalls cleaned. The kitchen, no longer content with meager gruel, began to produce wholesome, hearty meals, the scent of baking bread a welcome change from the usual stale air. Inmates were given clear tasks, their dignity restored through meaningful labor rather than idle confinement. Even the farmhouse itself seemed to lighten, scrubbed and aired until the lingering damp of neglect finally gave way.

The most remarkable transformation, however, was observed in Wesley. The man who had been a source of such terror to Ruth Haines, whose frustrations had often manifested in abrupt, unsettling "ebullitions," began to visibly change. Kneeland did not attempt to cage Wesley or force him into submission. Instead, he approached Wesley with a quiet, unwavering consistency, establishing routines, providing clean clothes that fit, and engaging him in simple, repetitive tasks that seemed to soothe his restless spirit. He spoke to Wesley with respect, not pity, and slowly, painstakingly, Wesley responded. The sharp, guttural sounds ceased. He began to eat his meals without incident, to follow instructions, even to offer a hesitant nod in acknowledgment. He ceased his disagreeable outbursts and now dressed and behaved like a civilized being. It was a testament to Kneeland's humane treatment, demonstrating that even those deemed "incorrigible" could respond to kindness and order. A sense of quiet industry, long absent, settled over the place like a comfortable blanket.

And then there was Ned. For years, the boy had been little more than a fixture in his bed under the eaves, his crippled leg a testament to neglect. Flint had scorned him, Haines had ignored him, and Clark had offered only useless pity. But Kneeland saw something more. He brought Ned new books, first. Then, cautiously, he began to work with him. It started with simple stretches in the morning, Ned's face a mask of pain, his breath hissing through clenched teeth. Kneeland would sit with him, his hand steady on Ned's twisted limb, guiding it through small, excruciating movements. Slowly, agonizingly, the stretches became more active exercises. Ned learned to pull himself up, first to a sitting position, then to stand for agonizing seconds, leaning heavily on the bed frame, his legs trembling violently. Each small gain was a monumental victory. There were setbacks, falls, days where the pain was too great and despair threatened to overwhelm him. But Kneeland was patient, unwavering, his quiet encouragement a steady current against the tide of Ned's doubt. Day by day, week by week, the strength returned, muscle by painstaking muscle, until the goal that had seemed an impossible dream began to flicker into real possibility: Ned Lakin, bed-ridden for years, might walk again.

Kneeland also had a particular interest in Edwin. He had observed the young man's quiet competence, his willingness to work, and the intelligence that gleamed in his eyes despite the drab uniform of an inmate. One evening, Kneeland called Edwin to his small office.

The oil lamp on Haskell Kneeland's desk cast a warm, steady glow, illuminating the neat stacks of ledgers and the worn leather binding of a town ordinance book. It was late, the Farm quiet save for the distant hoot of an owl. Kneeland sat upright, pen laid precisely beside an inkwell, as the faint rap at his door announced the arrival of Edwin.

Edwin entered cautiously, his usual reserved posture a little more rigid than usual. He had been summoned, and in his experience, summonses rarely heralded good news. He stood just inside the door, cap in hand, eyes deferentially cast towards the floorboards.

"Edwin," Kneeland began, his voice calm, "Come in, close the door. Have a seat." He gestured to the plain wooden chair opposite his desk.

Edwin hesitated, then slowly moved to the chair and sat on the very edge, his hands clasped tightly over his cap. He braced himself for a lecture, perhaps a new, more arduous task.

Kneeland observed him for a moment, then leaned forward, his shrewd eyes softening. "Edwin, I've had occasion to watch you these past months. Your diligence, your aptitude for honest labor, it hasn't gone unnoticed." He paused, then continued, "And I seem to recall, from records and whispers, that some years ago, you had an aspiration. An interest in a trade, was it not?"

Edwin's gaze flickered up, a flicker of surprise in his weary eyes. "Yes, sir," he mumbled, his voice a little hoarse. "A few years back. With Mr. Frost, the blacksmith here in Pondicherry." The memory felt like something from another lifetime, a foolish, forgotten dream.

A faint, almost imperceptible smile touched Kneeland's lips. "Just so. I've always held that the purpose of a Town Farm should be to rehabilitate or train inmates to be functioning members of society whenever possible, not merely to house them. And you, Edwin, have demonstrated the capacity for far more than merely existing within these walls."

Edwin's heart began a slow, hesitant thump against his ribs. A faint warmth, long dormant, spread through him. He dared not hope.

"I've recently had cause to speak with the Overseers of the Poor," Kneeland continued, his voice taking on a more formal, official tone. He gave a slight, almost imperceptible shake of his head. "And I've also had a lengthy discussion with Mr. Frost, the blacksmith."

Kneeland paused, letting the words hang in the quiet office. Edwin felt his breath catch in his throat.

"He has agreed, Edwin," Kneeland finally said, his voice clear and firm, "to take you on as an apprentice. You are to begin your apprenticeship with Mr. Frost, the blacksmith, here in Pondicherry."

For a long moment, Edwin could only stare. The words seemed to echo, disembodied, in the small room. *Apprenticeship. Mr. Frost. Freedom.* His mind, so long accustomed to the monotonous grind of servitude, struggled to grasp the sheer, improbable weight of it. "Sir?" he managed, his voice barely a whisper. "Truly? After all this time?"

Kneeland nodded, a genuine warmth now in his eyes. "Truly. It took some convincing, and certain obstacles seem to have... removed themselves from the path. The town feels as I do that your best use is to learn a trade to support yourself. That, and your dedication and diligence have made a most compelling case. The decision is made. You are to begin your apprenticeship."

A wave of overwhelming, almost painful gratitude washed over Edwin. His eyes welled, blurring the lamp's soft glow. He swallowed hard, trying to find words that felt adequate. "Sir... Mr. Kneeland... I... I don't know what to say." His voice trembled, a crack appearing in his carefully maintained composure. "Thank you. Thank you, sir. More than I can ever say."

Kneeland rose, walking around the desk to stand before Edwin. He placed a steady hand on the young man's shoulder. "Make the most of this, Edwin. Mr. Frost is a good man, and blacksmithing is a noble trade. This is your chance to build a life for yourself."

Edwin finally managed to stand, his whole body light with a hope he hadn't dared to feel in years. He could almost hear the clang of the hammer on the anvil, the roar of the forge, a sound of purposeful work, a sound of freedom. He clutched his cap tighter, nodding fiercely, a silent promise to seize this unexpected, miraculous opportunity.

For Edwin, the apprenticeship was a beacon of hard-won hope. But in the wider currents of Pondicherry, his newfound opportunity was about to sweep him directly into the path of Nat Libby's relentless ambition. Though Libby was no longer on the select board, his influence still cast a long shadow over town government. This decision, seemingly a simple act of rehabilitation, threatened to loosen his long-held grip on certain elements within Pondicherry. For Libby, the young man's freedom felt like a direct threat, a potential unraveling that could jeopardize his ambitious run for governor. The foundations of Libby's carefully constructed future had just been subtly, but significantly, shaken.

The door to Superintendent Kneeland's office clicked shut behind Edwin, and for a long moment, he simply stood in the dimly lit hallway, unmoving.

The world outside the warm circle of the lamp's glow seemed to hum with a strange, impossible quiet. The words echoed in his mind, not as a voice, but as a feeling, a sudden, explosive blossoming in his chest that threatened to overwhelm him.

His knees felt weak, and a gasp escaped his lips, sounding loud in the silence of the night. He reached out, his hand finding the cold, rough wall for support. A tremor ran through him, starting in his fingertips and shaking his whole frame. It wasn't the cold; it was the sudden, shattering release of years of stifled hope, of quiet despair, of a life he had thought was forever lost. A sob, raw and unexpected, tore from his throat. He clamped a hand over his mouth, burying his face in his palm, tears hot and sudden against his skin. He was going to be free. He was going to work for Mr. Frost, learning a trade, earning his own keep, living a life that wasn't bound by the Farm's oppressive routines.

He couldn't stay inside. The walls felt too close, too filled with the memories of what had been. His feet, as if guided by an instinct deeper than thought, turned towards the back door. He slipped out, past the sleeping form of the farmhouse, into the crisp night air. The stars glittered with an indifferent brilliance above, but to Edwin, they seemed to shimmer with a new, impossible light.

He walked quickly, almost stumbling, across the yard, past the silent barns and sheds, their dark forms hulking under the moon. He didn't think about where he was going, not consciously. His path was etched into his very being, worn by countless visits in times of quiet grief and desperate longing. He skirted the edge of the sprawling apple orchard, its gnarled branches reaching like skeletal fingers against the sky, their fruit long since harvested.

Beyond the orchard, where the land sloped gently away, lay the unmarked graves. A patch of ground, indistinguishable from any other to the uninitiated eye, yet to Edwin, it was consecrated earth. Here, under the rough Pondicherry soil, lay those who had died on the Farm, their identities often forgotten, their lives reduced to a few lines in a ledger, if even that. His mother was here. He knew her approximate resting place, a spot he had visited countless times in the deepest hours of the night, when the weight of his existence felt too heavy to bear.

He had been a newborn when she died. He remembered nothing of her face, nothing of her voice. All he knew was that she had died giving birth to him on this very farm, her brief life extinguished as his began. He was the reason she lay in this unmarked grave, and a part of him had always felt buried there with her, forever tied to this place. Now, on the precipice of his own hard-won freedom, he felt a profound, bittersweet sense of farewell to her lonely resting place, yet an undeniable, unending connection to her, and to the very ground of the Town Farm he was about to leave.

He didn't have to speak the words aloud; they flowed from his heart, a torrent of relief and sorrow and fierce determination. 'Ma,' the thought rasped through him, his internal voice hoarse with unshed tears, 'can you hear me? Did you see him? Mr. Kneeland. He did it, Ma. He's letting me go.'"

"I'm getting out, Ma." He swallowed, the imagined conversations, the tender moments of a childhood he never had, fading to the stark reality of his memory. "I'm going to be a blacksmith." His vow was not a shared dream, but a fiercely personal promise forged in the crucible of his longing. "I'll make something of myself."

A bitter sob caught in his throat. He thought of all the years lost, the indignities, the endless labor, the hopelessness. He thought of Flint's brutality, Obediah's ineffective kindness, Haines's crushing indifference. And then, Kneeland. A man who saw more than just an inmate, a burden, a pair of hands. A man who saw a person.

"It's not fair that you didn't get to see this, Ma. It's not fair you never got out." A fresh wave of tears flowed, burning tracks down his cold cheeks. But this time, they were different. Not just tears of sorrow, but tears of release, of a future unfolding.

He stayed there for a long time, the cold seeping into his bones, but he barely noticed. He poured out his heart to the silent grave, sharing his fear, his hope, his profound, dizzying sense of rebirth. When he finally stood, the first faint hint of dawn was bleeding into the eastern sky, painting the horizon in pale mauves and greys. The orchard seemed less skeletal now, touched by the promise of spring.

Edwin took a deep, shuddering breath. The air was cold, clean, and full of the scent of damp earth and distant woodsmoke. He felt lighter, as if a great weight had been lifted from his shoulders. He turned, not back towards the graves, but towards the faint, growing light, his gaze fixed on the unseen town beyond the hills, on Mr. Frost's smithy, on the life that finally, miraculously, awaited him. He would work hard. He would make the most of this. For himself, and for the memory of the mother who never had the chance.

That morning, the usual clatter of breakfast felt different to Edwin. Bleary-eyed from lack of sleep, he ate his porridge, still warm with the impossible glow of the previous night's news. He expected to be sent to the fields or the barn, but instead, Mrs. Kneeland approached him, her face kind.

"Edwin," she said softly, "you won't be doing chores today. Go pack your things."

Edwin's heart leaped. He nodded, unable to speak, and hurried to the small, shared room he'd occupied for as long as he could remember. His "things" amounted to little more than the worn clothes on his back and a few meager articles of spare clothing. He gathered them, folding them carefully, and placed them into the simple drawstring bag he used for laundry.

Reaching under his pillow, his fingers closed around a familiar, soft square of fabric. He pulled it out: the monogrammed handkerchief made for him by Nan. He held it, his rough fingertips tracing the awkward, endearing stitching of "E.L." The fabric was soft against his thumb, worn smooth by the years. A wave of bittersweet memory washed over him. He pictured Nan, Superintendent Sanborn's daughter, her face bright, her eyes sparkling with laughter, her lively chatter filling the dreary Farm with a much-needed warmth. She had been a beacon of sunshine, her cheerful disposition a balm to their weary souls. She'd been gone now for a long time, living life on her home farm as far as he knew. Her departure had left behind a silence that had never quite been filled.

He carefully tucked the handkerchief deep into his bag, a silent vow passing his lips. "I'm leaving, too, Nan," he whispered, his voice catching. "Finally, I'm leaving, too."

He carried his small bag downstairs, finding Superintendent Kneeland speaking quietly with a burly man by the kitchen door. The man was Mr. Frost, the blacksmith. He had arrived at the Farm on a twofold errand: to check on Nell, one of the farm's horses, who had unfortunately come up lame, and to give Edwin a ride to his house in the village.

Mr. Frost, a man with powerful shoulders and hands calloused from years at the forge, turned as Edwin approached. He offered a gruff but not unkind nod. "Ready, lad?" he asked, his voice surprisingly gentle.

Edwin nodded, his eyes wide with a mixture of apprehension and immense anticipation.

Superintendent Kneeland clapped Edwin on the shoulder. "He's ready, Mr. Frost. A good worker, keen to learn. You'll not regret it." He gave Edwin a final, encouraging look. "Remember what we spoke about, Edwin. This is your chance."

Edwin looked from Kneeland to Mr. Frost, then back to the familiar, worn entrance of the farmhouse. For the first time in his life, he felt like a free man with a purpose. He took a deep breath, the air tasting sharper, cleaner than it ever had before, and a tremor, both of excitement and profound loss, ran through him.

He was born on this farm. Every crooked fence post, every worn floorboard, every creak of the old house was etched into the very fabric of his memory. This was the only home he had ever known, the landscape of all his suffering, and all his small, unexpected joys. Though the years had been hard, marked by hardship and cruelty, there was a strange comfort in the familiar, even in its bleakness. Now, he was leaving it all behind—the grueling chores, the sparse meals, the fear of unpredictable superintendents, yes, but also the faces of those who remained, the quiet camaraderie with the other inmates, the simple routine of life he understood. He was stepping, finally, into the uncertain, promising expanse of his own future, a future thrilling in its possibility, yet terrifying in its unknown shape. He followed Mr. Frost out the door, a profound mix of excitement and sorrow swirling within him, leaving behind all that was known.

II

Part Two

"A man's true birthright is not the name he is given, but the name he earns through his deeds. The hands that were once bound by circumstance may be the same hands that forge a new foundation."
—Henry P. Stone, Pondicherry Chronicle, 1889

Chapter 18

The jingle of harness bells and the rhythmic clopping of Mr. Frost's mare, Daisy, were Edwin's first sounds of freedom. The air, crisp and carrying the faint scent of woodsmoke and pine, seemed to vibrate with a new energy as Mr. Frost's wagon rumbled away from the Town Farm. Edwin clutched his drawstring bag, the Nan handkerchief nestled deep inside, and risked a glance back. The familiar, grim outline of the farmhouse, his only home for as long as he could remember, grew smaller, then vanished behind a cluster of trees. A strange knot of both exhilaration and a profound, unexpected ache tightened in his chest. He was free, yes, but he was also adrift in a world entirely unknown.

For the initial stretch of the journey, the landscape unfolded as a familiar tapestry. They passed neat farms and sprawling fields, sights Edwin knew intimately. He'd been sent on countless errands to these very farms, hauling goods, mending fences, and lending his back to the arduous work of harvests. These were the boundaries of his known world, a world of dirt, sweat, and endless labor.

Then, as they approached the heart of the village, they passed the new church, its white steeple gleaming against the morning sky. Edwin knew this area well; he attended services here every Sunday. Across the street stood the schoolhouse, a place where he, like many other children from the Farm, had spent fleeting hours of education. This was the precise point where his familiar world ended.

From here on, the journey became a revelation. The road, a dusty track by the farm, transformed into a bustling thoroughfare lined with houses and shops. People moved with a purpose he rarely saw at the Farm, their laughter and calls carrying on the breeze. Carriages and wagons, more numerous and finer than any he'd seen regularly, passed them by, some at a brisk clip. Neighbors waved and exchanged greetings, a constant stream of life that made the isolated quiet of the Town Farm seem like a distant dream. Edwin, who had only ever known the quiet hum of farm life and the occasional passing traveler, stared with wide-eyed fascination. So much activity, so much going on, right on the very road!

Mr. Frost, sensing the young man's quiet awe, offered a low chuckle. "Aye, lad, the village is a mite livelier than the Farm. You'll get used to it."

They soon pulled into the yard of a substantial farmhouse, set close to the road. It wasn't just one house, Edwin noticed, but a series of connected structures: a large "big house" in the front, a "middle house" connecting it to a "back house," and finally, beyond that, the expansive barn. The air here was different, too—laced with the sharp, metallic tang of iron and the smoky scent of coal. The blacksmith's shop, a sturdy building with a wide, open door, stood just beyond the main cluster of the house, its forge a dark maw promising heat and noise.

Mr. Frost led Edwin through a side door of the middle house, stepping into a warm, inviting kitchen. A plump, kind-faced woman stood by a stove, stirring a pot, and a younger man, broad-shouldered like Mr. Frost, was repairing a harness by the window.

"Irene, Frank," Mr. Frost announced, "this here's Edwin. My new apprentice."

Irene Frost, his second wife and the widow of Lathrop March, turned, her smile immediate and genuine. "Welcome, Edwin! We've been expecting you." Her voice was soft, comforting. "It's good to have you."

Frank Frost, son of Mr. Frost and his first wife, Apphia, rose and offered a firm handshake. "Glad to have another pair of hands. Frank," he introduced himself, though Edwin had already guessed. "I'm a blacksmith too."

Soon after, a quiet woman with keen eyes, Lizzie, the household servant, emerged from a pantry, and a cheerful man named Martin, a 20-year-old son of a local farmer who served as a hired hand, came in from the yard. They offered nods of welcome, their presence adding to the unfamiliar faces and the comfortable, bustling atmosphere. Edwin was struck by the simple fact that these are people he would live and work with, day in and day out, in a place that felt undeniably like a home. The Frosts also had a grown daughter, Ida, who was married to William Fessenden and lived nearby, visiting often.

"Well, Edwin," Leander Frost said, his gaze appraising but kind. "Let's get you acquainted with the place."

He and Frank led Edwin on a thorough tour. They began with the blacksmith shop, the very heart of the operation. Inside, the forge glowed like a sleeping beast, still radiating residual warmth from the day's work. Hammers of various sizes hung neatly on pegs, their surfaces worn smooth with use, and the heavy anvil stood like a silent sentinel. The air, thick with the scent of coal smoke and burnt metal, was a stark contrast to the dust and animal odors of the Farm's barn. Edwin's eyes, wide with a quiet reverence, took in every detail, from the bellows to the racks of cooling horseshoes.

Next, they moved to the fields behind the house, sprawling and neatly fenced, hinting at a level of care and productivity Edwin hadn't often seen at the Farm. Leander pointed out the fallow ground, the spring plantings, and the distant woodlot that supplied their fuel. It was still agriculture, yes, but it felt different here—purposeful, managed.

Finally, they entered the barn, larger and better maintained than the one Edwin had known. The stalls were clean, the hay mounded high, and the air held a fresh, sweet scent. A sturdy workhorse whinnied a soft greeting. Edwin, accustomed to the raw conditions of the Town Farm barn, felt a quiet sense of respect for the order and care evident in every corner. This was not just work; it was a livelihood, tended with pride.

By the time they returned to the kitchen, the aroma of supper was thick in the air. The long kitchen table, heavy and scrubbed clean, groaned under the weight of an unfamiliar bounty. Platter after platter emerged from the pantry and stove: a roast chicken, golden and glistening, bowls mounded with mashed potatoes and green beans glistening with butter, a steaming loaf of fresh bread, and even a tart crowned with sweetened berries for dessert. At the Farm, meals were plain, rationed, and meant only to fuel, never to please.

Here, the sheer abundance was a revelation. The aroma alone, a complex symphony of roasting meat and baking bread, made Edwin's stomach clench with an unfamiliar mixture of anticipation and disbelief.

He ate alongside the family and the hired help, a stark contrast to the segregated, silent meals at the Farm. The flavors danced on his tongue, each bite richer than anything he'd ever known, and the portions seemed limitless. He ate slowly, savoring each mouthful, but found himself shy to take more than usual, despite his hunger, so ingrained was the habit of scarcity.

Mr. Frost, noticing his hesitation as he reached for a second slice of bread, chuckled low. "Don't be shy, lad! Dig in! We've plenty here."

Irene, with a kind, reassuring smile, added, "That's right, Edwin. I didn't make it to throw it out! Help yourself."

Encouraged, Edwin allowed himself to fill his plate a little more, the warmth of the food and the company settling a new kind of contentment in his belly.

After the hearty meal, Irene Frost showed Edwin to his room. It was up the steep stairs in the middle house, a small room, simply furnished with a bed, a chest of drawers, and a narrow window that looked out over the garden. Beyond the garden, set back from the road, was the blacksmith shop

Mrs. Frost, bustling about, making sure everything was tidy and welcoming, chattered, "You'll enjoy this room in the winter, Edwin. It's always warm from the kitchen below." Satisfied that all was in order, she said, "Well, I'll leave you to get settled, then." With a warm smile, she left, pulling the sturdy, wooden door shut behind her.

Edwin stood looking around the room, amazed. This was his room. His own room. After sharing cramped spaces with Ned, Wesley, and countless other inmates for all his life, the privacy was a luxury beyond imagining. He set his drawstring bag on the bed. This was real.

He sat on the edge of the bed, slowly, as if testing its reality. The mattress, though simple, felt softer than anything he'd known at the Farm. He ran a hand over the smooth wood of the chest of drawers. Every surface here spoke of permanence, of being cared for. He stood and walked to the window, peering out at the moonlit garden, the silhouette of the blacksmith shop a comforting bulk against the night sky. The road beyond, which had bustled with life earlier, was now hushed, save for the distant bark of a dog or the faint creak of a wagon in the wind.

He climbed into bed, pulling the new, soft quilt—so unlike the thin, scratchy blankets of the Farm—up to his chin. The silence of the room was profound, almost deafening. At the Farm, there was always something: Ned's restless shifting, Wesley's soft, even snores, the murmur of distant voices from other parts of the house, the creak of floorboards under unseen steps. Here, there was just the quiet hum of the night, the faint whisper of wind through the eaves.

He closed his eyes, and images drifted through his mind. Not the grimness of the Farm, not exactly. Instead, he saw Ned's mischievous grin as they'd snuck him an extra potato, heard Wesley's chortling laugh that always made him laugh, too. A pang, sharp and unexpected, tightened in his chest. He missed them. Missed the familiar weight of their sleeping forms near his own, the shared hardship that had forged an unspoken bond. They were still there, in that dim, overcrowded room, while he was here, in this quiet, private space. A wave of guilt, brief but potent, washed over him, quickly followed by a powerful relief.

He thought of the abundance on the supper table, the kindness in Irene's eyes, the firm, honest handshake of Frank. He thought of the blacksmith shop, the smell of coal, the promise of purpose. He felt the vastness of the village, stretching out beyond his window, a world he was only just beginning to truly see.

The quiet, once unsettling, slowly began to feel like a balm. The unfamiliar bed cradled him. The sounds of the Farm faded, replaced by the gentle rhythm of his own breathing. He was Edwin Littlefield, Apprentice, no longer an inmate. And as the thoughts softened, drifting like smoke, he succumbed to the deepest, most peaceful sleep he'd known in years.

The next morning, his apprenticeship began. Mr. Frost did not immediately set him to the forge. Instead, he started Edwin with the fundamentals, building a foundation of discipline and observation. Edwin's duties were basic: sweeping the shop floor, keeping it clear of scraps of iron and coal dust, fetching wood and coal from the sheds, and, most importantly, learning to operate the great leather bellows that fed air to the forge. He quickly learned the rhythm of the work: the whoosh of the bellows, the roar of the fire, the clang of hammer on anvil from Mr. Frost and Frank as they worked on horseshoes and wagon wheels.

The shop itself was a symphony of creation. Sparks danced in the dim light, the smell of burnt coal and hot metal filled the air, and the constant clang of hammers was a vibrant, living sound that spoke of strength and purpose. Edwin watched, fascinated, as raw iron, red-hot from the forge, yielded to the smiths' powerful blows, transforming into intricate shapes. This was not the mindless, repetitive labor of the Farm. This was a craft, a skill, and Edwin felt a deep, instinctive pull towards it. He was a quick study, his years of farm labor having granted him a sturdy build and a quiet diligence. He swept with methodical precision, fetched wood without complaint, and soon mastered the rhythmic pumping of the bellows, keeping the fire alive and roaring.

The days passed, each one a step further from the Farm. Edwin was still quiet, still learning the subtle cues of his new surroundings, but a lightness had begun to settle over him. He was no longer just Edwin, the nameless inmate. He was Edwin, the apprentice, a part of the Frost household, learning a trade that hummed with life and purpose. And from the window of his own room in the middle house, he could see the constant stream of life on the main road, a reminder that the world was vast and full of movement, and he, finally, was moving with it.

One afternoon, a few days after his arrival, Edwin watched as Mr. Frost led Daisy, his own beautiful mare, into the shop. Daisy was a sight to behold: a glossy black horse with a spirited step and intelligent eyes, a stark contrast to the weary workhorses of the Farm. Mr. Frost was checking her shoes, tapping them gently with a small hammer.

"She's a fine animal, Mr. Frost," Edwin ventured, his voice still a little hesitant.

Mr. Frost smiled, stroking Daisy's sleek neck. "That she is, lad. My best. My pride and joy, she is." He looked at Edwin, then nodded towards a worn bucket of tools. "Fetch me the hoof pick, Edwin. And then, hold her lead steady. Gentle, mind you. She knows a kind hand."

Edwin carefully retrieved the tool. As he approached Daisy, her dark eye watched him, but she stood calmly. He reached out, his fingers surprisingly steady as he gripped her lead. He felt the immense power in the mare's body, the warmth of her coat, and for the first time, he felt a part of something alive and vibrant, not merely enduring. He held her, focused, feeling the subtle shifts of her weight as Mr. Frost worked, and a quiet sense of pride bloomed in his chest. This was learning. This was purpose.

Chapter 19

The days at the Frost household settled into a rhythm that, for Edwin, was both demanding and deeply satisfying. The clang of the forge, the scent of coal and hot iron, the steady guidance of Mr. Frost and Frank – it was a world away from the aimless drudgery of the Town Farm. He was learning, truly learning, and the knowledge felt like a tangible thing, something he could hold in his hands and shape, just like the metal.

One warm Saturday evening, the Frost kitchen was a hive of activity. The air was thick with the sweet, tangy smell of ripe tomatoes, the heat from the woodstove compounding the summer warmth. Irene Frost, her face flushed and her apron stained with tomato juice, bustled about with Ida Fessenden, her daughter, engaged in the hot, laborious task of "putting up" tomatoes for the winter. Ida's children helped by washing the tomatoes in the big farm sink in the pantry. It was a very busy time, full of clattering jars and hushed instructions.

"Edwin, dear," Irene called out, her voice still gentle despite the work, "would you be a lamb and take these tomatoes to Widow Barker? Her rheumatism has been acting up, and she's partial to my early crop." She handed him a small basket, heavy with ripe, red fruit, still warm from the sun-drenched garden.

"Yes, ma'am," Edwin replied, a pleasant warmth spreading through him. An errand for Mrs. Frost was a welcome task, a small sign of trust, and the walk through the village was always a chance to observe the bustling life he was now a part of. He set off, whistling a tuneless melody, enjoying the feel of the sun on his face and the gentle weight of the basket.

He walked up over Minister's Hill, his calves complaining. He passed the parsonage, waving to Mrs. Hague who was already at work in her kitchen garden, her back bent over neat rows of greens. He turned onto the quiet lane where Widow Barker lived, her cozy home nestled among overgrown lilac bushes. He delivered the tomatoes, exchanged a few polite words, and then turned back down the quiet lane. As he walked back down the hill, whistling. Then, he saw him.

A young man, moving with a steady, if slightly uneven, gait, was sweeping the walkway in front of Knapp & Sanborn's general store. His frame was still thin, but his shoulders held a new breadth, and his head was lifted, not bent. Edwin stopped dead, the whistle dying on his lips. He blinked, hardly daring to believe his eyes, his mind struggling to reconcile this purposeful figure with the bed-ridden boy he remembered. The familiar shock of dark hair, the sharp, intelligent profile....

"Ned?" Edwin called out, his voice thick with disbelief and a sudden surge of warmth.

The young man paused, his broom resting against the storefront. He turned, and a wider, brighter smile than Edwin had ever seen on his face spread across it, transforming his features. "Edwin! Well, I'll be! Look at me!" Ned took a step forward, a triumphant gesture. "Mr. Kneeland, he did it! He made me walk again!"

Edwin found himself grinning, a genuine, joyful expression he hadn't realized he was capable of. He quickly covered the distance between them, clapping Ned firmly on the shoulder. "Ned, I... I never thought... It's a miracle!"

"No miracle, just stubbornness and Mr. Kneeland's patience," Ned chuckled, his eyes shining. "Been helping Mr. Knapp here with sweeping and stocking shelves. It's not much, but it's work. And I can stand to do it." He gestured proudly with the broom.

"I can see that," Edwin murmured, still amazed. He looked at his friend, truly seeing him for the first time in years – not the invalid, but a young man, upright and independent. The changes were profound, a testament to resilience Edwin was only just beginning to understand.

After a few more excited exchanges, catching up on each other's news, Edwin finally continued on his way to the Frosts' house, returning to the sounds of simmering pots and the comforting voices of the family still at work in the kitchen, but with a lighter step and a newfound sense of wonder.

That same Saturday night, after the household had finally settled and the lights in the Frosts' farmhouse had dimmed, a figure moved with practiced stealth around the back of Ida Fessenden's newly purchased property. The house, located just north of the old Parson Fessenden place, sat quiet under the shroud of darkness. A faint click, then the almost imperceptible scrape of metal against wood. The key, left innocently in the inside lock as was Ida's habit, was nudged, a dull thud signaling its fall to the floor. A moment later, a different click, a faint resistance, then the soft turning of a tumbler. The back door, which Ida had secured, swung inward just enough for a slim form to slip through.

Inside, the intruder moved with purpose. No fumbling, no unnecessary noise. Direct to the bedroom, to the bureau. A drawer opened, then another. The sound of fabric rustling, a small leather item being lifted. Then, a pause. A glint of gold in the dim light was noted, then bypassed. The drawer was gently closed. The figure slipped back to the open back door, closing it silently behind them, leaving the fallen key on the floor where it lay. The night resumed its quiet.

The next morning, on Sunday, when Ida returned to her own house, the front door was as she had left it. She stepped inside, the familiar quiet of her home greeting her. But as she moved through the small parlor, a subtle disarray caught her eye. A curtain seemed to hang slightly askew. A chair was not quite where she remembered it. A prickle of unease ran down her spine.

She walked towards the back of the house, her heart beginning to beat a little faster. The back door, which she had locked so carefully, stood ajar. On the floor just inside, glinting dully, lay the key she had left in the lock.

A cold dread settled over her. She rushed to the bureau drawer where she kept her valuables. Her breath hitched. The small leather pocket-book was gone. Seventy dollars, vanished. Her hands trembled as she rummaged through the drawer. Then, a gasp of confusion escaped her. Her nice gold watch, its delicate chain, and other pieces of jewelry, worth a considerable twenty-five dollars, lay untouched, exactly as she had left them. The thief had been selective. Someone who knew what to take, and what to leave behind, perhaps fearing that easily identified items might lead to their capture. The quiet violation of her home, the methodical nature of the theft, sent a shiver of fear through her. Who would do such a thing? Who knew her habits, her home, so intimately?

The news of the burglary spread through Pondicherry like wildfire, igniting a sensation that eclipsed even the recent troubles at the Town Farm. A theft, in their quiet, orderly village! And seventy dollars, a small fortune! The *Pondicherry Chronicle* would later capture the village's shock:

"Pondicherry has had the unusual sensation of a burglary. Last Saturday night Mrs. Ida Fessenden, who, with her children occupies her new purchase, the property north of the Parson Fessenden place, stopped over night at the home of her step-father and mother, Mr. and Mrs. Leander Frost. Next morning on entering her house she found evidence that it had been visited during her absence, and on opening a bureau drawer where she left her money and other valuables, found that her pocket-book with its contents, seventy dollars, was gone. Singularly enough, her nice watch and gold chain and other jewelry to the value of twenty-five dollars, were there, just as she left them. On unfastening the back door, she found the key, which she had left in the lock, after locking the door on the inside, lay on the floor; which went to show that the burglar had entered by that door, by pushing at the key and then unlocking the door with a false key. It is highly probable that the thief was some one well acquainted with the premises, and the seemingly strange fact of leaving the watch and jewelry intact can be accounted for on no other theory than the fear that the possession of those easily identified articles might someway lead to detection. So far the perpetrator of the deed is enshrouded in mystery, but it is hoped that full light on the matter may soon dawn. The affair, as it may well be supposed, has caused much excitement in that quiet village."

The "mystery" did not remain shrouded for long, at least not in the minds of many Pondicherry residents. Ida Fessenden, distraught and angry, immediately thought of Edwin. He had been on an errand earlier that very day, walking right past her house. He was new to the village, a former inmate of the Town Farm, a place notorious for its "unruly" residents and questionable characters. He had no family, no history in the town, a blank slate onto which suspicion could easily be painted. Perhaps it was some passing tramp, one of the many boxcar wanderers brought to town by the railway, but Edwin was right here, accessible, and known to be from "the Farm."

Ida marched straight to the blacksmith shop, her face flushed with indignation. She found Edwin sweeping the shop floor, his brow furrowed in concentration. "You!" she accused, her voice sharp, pointing a trembling finger at him. "You were out yesterday, weren't you? Walking right by my house! My money is gone, and you're the only one who fits!"

Edwin froze, the broom clattering to the floor with a hollow clang that echoed the sudden emptiness in his chest. The accusation, so sudden and venomous, struck him not just as a blow, but as an impossible, absurd claim. A hot wave of shame and disbelief washed over him, chilling him even as his face flushed. His mind reeled. "Ma'am?" he stammered, his voice thin. "I... I was taking tomatoes to Widow Burnham, just as Mrs. Frost asked."

Mr. Frost, who had been hammering at the forge, let his hammer fall silent. The sudden quiet in the shop was deafening. He walked over, his face grim. "Edwin," he said, his voice low, "Ida's upset. Tell me the truth, lad. Did you have anything to do with this?"

Edwin met Mr. Frost's gaze, his own eyes wide and earnest. He saw the grimness there, the flicker of doubt, and a fresh wave of hurt washed over him. "No, sir! I swear it! I would never!" His voice trembled with a mixture of shock and betrayal. It was the familiar burn of judgment, igniting the old, familiar ache of being branded an outsider.

But the seed of suspicion had been planted, and it took root with astonishing speed. As Edwin walked through the village in the days that followed, the change was palpable, chilling. The polite nods he'd grown accustomed to vanished, replaced by averted gazes, by eyes that darted away when he met them, or worse, narrowed with undisguised judgment. Whispers followed him like a physical shadow, hushed tones that ceased abruptly the moment he drew near, leaving behind a heavy, silent accusation. He felt the weight of their judgment, the easy assumption of guilt based solely on his past, on the stain of the Town Farm. He was the outsider, the unknown quantity, and therefore, the convenient suspect.

Indeed, Haskell Kneeland, the Town Farm Superintendent, heard the rumors, and his brow furrowed with a familiar, righteous indignation. This was precisely the kind of baseless prejudice he fought against. He didn't just hear the whispers; he felt the injustice settle cold on his own skin. Without hesitation, he sought out the Selectmen, his voice measured but firm, laying out his conviction. Then, he took his stand publicly, speaking to anyone who would listen in the town square and at the general store. "Edwin is an honest, diligent young man," he declared, his voice cutting through the murmurs, leaving no room for doubt. "He has proven his character. To accuse him without proof is a grave injustice." His words, carrying the undeniable weight of his respected reputation, did more than offer a small counter-current; they challenged the very foundation of the town's hasty judgment, making some pause and others look away in discomfort.

Despite the inquiries and the quiet efforts of some, the actual perpetrator of the deed remained "enshrouded in mystery," as the *Chronicle* had put it. The money was gone, and the village had no answers. And so, the suspicion, though never officially declared, lingered over Edwin like a persistent cloud. The quickness with which the town had turned on him, their willingness to see the worst, confirmed a bitter truth. He might be free from the physical confines of the Farm, but the stigma, the mark of his origins, would always follow him. He was still an outsider, and the realization drove home his profound sense of not belonging, a bitter, cold truth that settled deep in his bones. It was a wound that would take far longer to heal than any physical bruise.

Chapter 20

The lingering shadow of the unresolved burglary at Ida Fessenden's house clung to Edwin. He kept his head down, focused on his work at the forge, allowing the clang of hammer on iron to drown out the whispers that followed him like a persistent fly. Mr. Frost, though he never spoke of it again, offered a steady presence, his gruff instructions a form of unspoken trust. Irene Frost continued to serve him generous portions at the dinner table, her kind eyes offering a comfort that bypassed words. But outside the safe haven of the Frosts' home and shop, the village remained a place of sidelong glances and hushed conversations. The knowledge that he was so easily deemed a suspect, simply for being who he was and where he came from, burned a slow, hurtful fire within him. It was a brand, invisible but real, singeing away the fragile hope of truly belonging. No amount of hard work or good intentions, it seemed, could ever truly erase the mark of the Town Farm.

One Sunday, after church service at the new church, a familiar voice called his name.

"Edwin! Is that really you?"

He turned, and his breath caught, a sudden, unexpected jolt running through him. Standing there, bathed in the soft Sunday light, a vision in a smartly tailored dress, was Nan Sanborn. For a fleeting moment, the weight of the town's judgment lifted, replaced by the sheer, improbable joy of seeing a face from a time when he was just a boy. It had been three years since he'd last seen her, three long years since her parents, Amos and Dorcas

Sanborn, the former Superintendent and Matron, had left the Town Farm. When they departed, Edwin had been a raw-boned fifteen-year-old boy, and Nan a vivacious twelve-year-old girl who had brought bursts of laughter and unexpected kindness to the bleak existence of the Farm inmates.

Now, at fifteen, Nan was growing into a striking young woman. Her eyes still held that familiar sparkle, but there was a new poise, a refined air about her. He remembered her boundless energy, her bright curiosity, and the way she'd once made him a handkerchief with his initials, a treasured possession he still kept.

"Nan," he managed, his voice a little hoarse, "You've grown so much."

She laughed, a delightful, unburdened sound. "And you, Edwin, look… well, different. Stronger, somehow. Mr. Frost's apprentice, I hear! That's wonderful!"

Nan's enthusiasm was infectious. "I've had lots of changes, too! I'm attending Gorham Seminary on a scholarship, you know," she began, her words tumbling out in a joyful rush. "It's simply marvelous, Edwin! We study so many fascinating things—Latin, mathematics, literature! And the debates! Oh, you should hear them. There are girls from all over Maine, and so many of them are from families right here in Pondicherry. I've become quite good friends with the Abbotts' daughter, Eliza, and young Miss Chandler, whose father owns the lumber mill. It's a very different world from the Farm, as you can imagine!" She paused, her gaze sweeping over Edwin, taking in his strong frame, his quiet demeanor. "And you, a blacksmith! That's real work, honest work. I'm so glad things are going well for you here."

Then, her eyes brightened even further, sparkling with an almost childlike wonder. Her voice softened, taking on a dreamy quality. "And then there's Simon Libby." She leaned in slightly, as if sharing a secret. "He's two years ahead of me at the Seminary, and, Edwin, he's simply marvelous! He has his father's charisma, you know, Senator Libby? Simon is so charming, and he truly understands me. He showers me with the most thoughtful gifts and compliments, and he talks about the future, about how we could make a difference!"

Her parents, Amos and Dorcas, watched from a polite distance, their expressions a mix of pride and a subtle, unreadable concern. They had heard rumors, whispers about both Senator Nat Libby and his son, Simon—stories of inappropriate behavior with women, of a casual disregard for others. But faced with Nan's obvious happiness, her radiant joy, they had, for now, given way to her youthful enthusiasm, a silent prayer on Dorcas's lips that this might indeed be the way to a better life, even as a flicker of concern remained in Amos's gaze. They wanted their daughter to be happy, to have a better life than the hardscrabble existence they'd known.

Meanwhile, Senator Nat Libby was far from pleased. He had envisioned Simon marrying the daughter of one of Pondicherry's leading citizens, a match that would solidify alliances and further their political ambitions. A farmer's daughter, even one as bright and charming as Nan, was not part of his plan. The Senator and Simon argued bitterly about it.

A few weeks later, the tension became palpable during a dinner at the Libby mansion on Main Hill. Senator Nat Libby had specifically invited Nan to dine with them, her parents notably absent. He had known her since she was a girl, due to his dealings with the Town Farm and her father, Amos, the former superintendent. But as she sat across from him now, a captivating young woman with an undeniable grace, his demeanor shifted.

"My dear Nan," Senator Libby began, his voice a practiced purr that was just a shade too smooth. He leaned forward slightly, his eyes never leaving hers. "It's truly a delight to see you again. My, how time transforms a sweet girl into... well, into such a radiant young woman. Gorham Seminary has clearly done wonders, though I suspect the true credit lies with nature's own hand." He paused, a faint, indulgent smile playing on his lips. "Simon speaks of you often, of course. His admiration is quite transparent. And I confess, seeing you here, I quite understand why." He raised his glass slightly, his gaze lingering on her. His gaze, she noticed, lingered a moment too long, a possessive gleam in his eyes. "You have a certain spark, a quiet strength that is quite captivating, my dear. A young woman with your qualities... you are destined for great things, I can see it." His words, though seemingly complimentary, carried an undercurrent that made Nan feel both flattered and vaguely uncomfortable, a sensation she couldn't quite place. A prickle of unease traced its way down her spine, like a cold draft in a warm room. She felt her smile tighten, a subtle shift in her posture, a subconscious desire to shrink just a fraction under his intense scrutiny.

Mrs. Libby sat silent, her lips drawn in disapproval.

When his parents had left the table, Simon leaned in and took Nan's hand in his. "I want to apologize for my father. Too much brandy. He gets a bit inappropriate sometimes when he's in his cups." He leaned in and kissed her gently on the cheek. He looked hopefully into her face. She smiled at him, a faint blush still on her cheeks, but a sliver of that earlier unease remained, a seed of doubt his kiss couldn't quite erase. "Your father... he certainly is a powerful man," she said, choosing her words carefully, still processing the strange mixture of flattery and unease.

When Nan returned home that evening, her mother, Dorcas, was waiting up, a shawl wrapped around her shoulders. "Well, dearie? How was the evening?" she asked, her voice eager.

Nan launched into a breathless account of the grand house, the fine food, and Simon's charming attentiveness. When she mentioned Senator Libby's compliments, a pleased smile touched Dorcas's lips. "He sounds... very taken with you, Nan. And why shouldn't he be? You were made for finer things than sweating over a hot stove or mucking out barns like your old mother. You'd never have to do such hard physical labor if you married into a family like the Libbys." Dorcas, having spent years toiling at the Town Farm and now on their own small farm, was beginning to see the immense advantages this match could bring her beloved daughter. She yearned for a life for Nan free from the aching back and calloused hands that had marked her own existence. Nan had beauty and grace; she was meant for a life of comfort and influence, not endless back-breaking work.

Amos Sanborn, however, who had come in from checking on the livestock, listened with a more somber expression. He leaned against the doorframe, his gaze thoughtful as Nan chattered on. He knew men, and he knew the seamier side of life that the Town Farm had exposed him to. He'd seen how power could corrupt, how charm could mask darker intentions. "Finer things, aye," he grunted, a skeptical note in his voice. "Just make sure those finer things don't come with a hidden cost, Nan. Not all that glitters is gold, especially when it comes to politicians and their sons." His misgivings, born of hard experience, lingered in the air, a stark contrast to Dorcas's burgeoning hopes.

Chapter 21

The news of Nan Sanborn's engagement to Simon Libby had rippled through the village, a story of unexpected social ascent. For a farmer's daughter, even one as bright and graceful as Nan, to marry into the powerful Libby family was a testament to her charm and Simon's surprising choice. After protracted arguments, even Senator Nat Libby had reluctantly, if calculatingly, given his consent, seeing perhaps a different kind of political advantage in acquiring a beautiful, unblemished bride for his ambitious son.

The day of the wedding dawned clear and bright, a perfect late summer afternoon. The new church, usually a place of quiet reverence, buzzed with an almost palpable excitement. Carriages lined the street, their polished surfaces gleaming, depositing Pondicherry's elite, dressed in their finest silks and broadcloth. The air hummed with hushed chatter and the rustle of expensive fabrics.

Inside, the church was transformed. Every pew was adorned with delicate white ribbons, tied in elaborate bows. Great sprays of white lilies and roses, interspersed with fragrant ferns and orange blossoms—grown specially for the occasion in Nat Libby's greenhouse—graced the altar and filled the air with their perfume. Sunlight streamed through the tall stained-glass windows, casting jewel-toned patterns across the polished wooden floors.

Edwin sat with the Frosts in their pew towards the back of the church, observing the spectacle. He watched the grand procession begin, the pipe organ swelling to fill the space with majestic chords.

Then, Nan appeared.

She wore a magnificent white satin gown, a vision of bridal elegance. The fabric shimmered as she moved, draped over a bustle and trailing into a long train. Her bodice was intricately fashioned, adorned with delicate lace at the neckline and cuffs. A long, sheer veil flowed from a small tiara of orange blossoms nestled in her hair, obscuring her face ever so slightly, adding to her ethereal beauty. In her hands, she carried a small bouquet of white flowers, tied with matching ribbons. She looked every inch the society bride, radiant and graceful, perfectly embodying the "finer things" her mother, Dorcas, had so desperately wished for her.

Simon Libby stood at the altar, impeccably dressed in a dark suit, his handsome face radiating a practiced charm. He exuded confidence, his smile wide and inviting as Nan approached. He was the picture of a devoted groom, his future political aspirations already seeming to shine around him like an aura.

The ceremony proceeded with all the solemnity and tradition of the time. The vows were exchanged, their voices clear and firm. Simon slipped a gold band onto Nan's finger, a symbol of their union. The minister delivered a heartfelt sermon on love and devotion, his words echoing in the hushed church.

From his seat, Edwin watched Nan, a flicker of something unreadable in his own eyes. He saw the genuine happiness on her face, the almost-too-bright glow, and remembered the Nan who had been kind to him at the Farm. He then glanced at her parents, Amos and Dorcas Sanborn. Dorcas, seated proudly in the front row, dabbed at her eyes with a lace handkerchief, her face a mixture of joyous pride and awe at her daughter's ascent. Amos, beside her, maintained a more guarded expression. He nodded politely to well-wishers, but his gaze often strayed to Simon, a quiet skepticism lingering in his weathered eyes. He knew his daughter was beautiful and good, but he also knew the world, and the powerful men who moved within it, often had hidden depths.

Senator Nat Libby sat with his plump wife, front and center, a picture of patriarchal satisfaction. His gaze, however, lingered on Nan with a possessive air that was more than mere paternal pride. This marriage was a strategic triumph, a perfectly cast role for his son, and a beautiful acquisition for the family. The political machinations behind the scenes were now, outwardly, resolved into this pristine, public display of domestic harmony and rising influence. A faint, self-satisfied smile played on his lips as if the entire event were a carefully orchestrated performance, and he, the master puppeteer, was finally enjoying his masterpiece.

Finally, with a pronouncement, Simon and Nan were declared husband and wife. The church erupted in applause, and the new Mr. and Mrs. Simon Libby turned, walking back down the aisle, their faces alight, bathed in the joyous celebration of their union. Nan seemed to step into a new world, one of wealth and status, leaving behind the simpler life she once knew. The doors of the church opened, spilling light and newly wedded bliss onto the sun-drenched street, into a future that held both glittering promise and an undercurrent of unspoken complexities. The sweet scent of lilies and orange blossoms, now mingling with the celebratory buzz of the crowd, seemed to carry a subtle, bittersweet note, a faint echo of promises made and perhaps, costs yet unknown.

Chapter 22

Life at the forge had found its rhythm, a comforting cadence for Edwin amidst the unsettling undercurrents of the village. The rhythmic clang of hammer on anvil, the roar of the bellows, the scent of coal and hot iron – these were his anchors. He was learning, truly learning, absorbing the subtle nuances of metalwork under Leander Frost's watchful eye. He was no longer just an apprentice; his hands grew stronger, his judgment sharper, his understanding of the craft deepening with each passing week. He began to feel a burgeoning sense of purpose, a quiet pride in the skills he was acquiring.

Yet, a new shadow began to creep into the forge, subtle at first, then undeniably present. Leander Frost, already lame from an old accident, began to struggle more noticeably with his leg. When he was a young man, in the days before the war, he and some neighbors had been digging a well. They were using explosives to clear rock, and a terrible miscalculation, an accidental explosion, had blown Leander clear out of the well. His hand had been badly injured, but it was his leg that had taken the brunt of the blast, left in terrible shape. The doctor, seeing the mangled limb, had told him sternly that the leg would have to come off. Leander, a man of fierce resolve, had famously replied, "If my leg is going, I'm going with it!" The doctor, against all odds, had managed to save the leg, but the pain from that injury had been a constant, grinding companion for Leander's entire life.

Before the war, the forge had been a bustling place. Leander had his son, Frank, to help, a strong and capable smith in his own right. And there was also his nephew, Arthur Jordan, a promising young man who had pitched in, learning the trade alongside his cousin. But Arthur had answered the call of duty, joining the Union Army, and the war had claimed him. He'd been severely wounded at the Battle of Cedar Mountain, captured, and endured the horrors of Belle Isle prisoner of war camp. Though he was part of a prisoner exchange, Arthur died soon after, succumbing to his injuries. Frank had returned unscathed, a blessing they never took for granted, but the loss of Arthur, so full of life and promise, still haunted them both, a silent void in the shop and in their hearts.

In Edwin, both Leander and Frank saw someone who could fill that void – if not emotionally, then certainly for the continuation of the family business. Edwin was quick, strong, and possessed a quiet dedication. He was learning the trade with a speed that pleased Leander.

As the months passed, Leander's growing lameness became undeniable. The pain etched itself deeper into his face, and his movements grew slower, more deliberate. One autumn, driven by a desperate hope that a change of climate might ease his suffering, Leander decided to take the train West. His devoted wife, Irene, accompanied him. They were gone for weeks, a quiet and anxious period for Frank and Edwin at the forge.

Then, a telegram arrived. It was brief, sparse on details, but the message was clear: Leander was not improving. His journey had not brought healing, but rather a somber realization. He knew, with the certainty of a man facing his end, that he didn't have long to live.

Leander and Irene returned home, their trip West curtailed. The journey back was slow, painful. Leander spent his final days in the house he had built with his own hands in 1870, surrounded by the familiar sounds of his home and, faintly, the distant clang of the forge. He passed away peacefully, leaving behind a profound stillness in the house and a deep void in the heart of his family.

His death left Frank and Edwin with a heavy responsibility. The forge, the business, the legacy of Leander Frost now rested squarely on their shoulders. Edwin, still mourning the man who had given him a new life, understood the gravity of their situation. He had progressed enough in his trade, his skills honed by Leander's patient instruction, that he was ready to step up. He was no longer just an apprentice; he was now a journeyman, capable of working independently, his own hammer ready to ring on the anvil. The continuation of the forge depended on him, on them both. The blacksmith shop, once bustling with three men, now looked to two to carry on its vital work.

The days following Leander Frost's funeral were draped in a somber quiet. The clatter of the forge seemed muted, as if even the iron mourned the master's passing. Frank, now the undisputed head of the household and the business, carried the weight of grief with a grim determination. His jaw was often set, his eyes holding a faraway look that spoke of memories and the sudden, overwhelming burden. Edwin felt it too, a dull ache beneath his ribs, a sense of loss for the man who had pulled him from the bleakness of the Town Farm and taught him a trade.

One evening, after supper, as Irene retired early, Frank called Edwin into the quiet sitting room. The air felt heavy with unspoken thoughts.

"Edwin," Frank began, his voice rougher than usual, "Father's gone. And with him, a good deal of the strength in this shop." He paused, running a hand over his tired face. "You've grown into a fine smith, lad. A true journeyman now. Most men your age, with your skill, would be looking to move on. To travel, work in different shops, learn new methods. That's the way of it for a journeyman, isn't it?"

Edwin nodded slowly. The thought had, indeed, crossed his mind. The open road, the chance to see more of the world, to test his skills against new challenges – it held a certain allure, a distant echo of the freedom he now possessed. A journeyman, by tradition, was a traveling craftsman, perfecting his trade before settling down, perhaps to become a master himself.

"But," Frank continued, meeting Edwin's gaze, "the forge needs you, Edwin. I need you. Father built this place with his hands, and Arthur... Arthur would have been here." His voice hitched slightly at his brother's name. "We can't let it falter now. Not with him gone."

Edwin looked around the familiar room, at the worn armchair where Leander often sat, at the framed silhouette on the mantelpiece. This house, this shop, this family—despite the recent suspicion from the town—had become the closest thing to home he had ever known. Here, he was not merely an inmate or a number; he was Edwin, the apprentice, now the journeyman, a respected part of a working enterprise. He remembered the cold, impersonal walls of the Town Farm, the endless, meaningless toil. Here, every strike of his hammer contributed to something real, something valuable.

"I won't leave you, Frank," Edwin said, his voice steady, surprising even himself with its conviction. "We'll carry it on. Together."

A wave of relief washed over Frank's face, softening the lines of grief and worry. A genuine, grateful smile touched his lips, a rare sight in these somber days. "Good, Edwin. Good. I knew I could count on you."

And so, Edwin committed to the forge, delaying the traditional wanderings of a journeyman for a time, yet knowing his growing skill might eventually call him to new ventures. For now, he would deepen his mastery right here in Pondicherry, taking on more responsibility, learning to manage the business alongside Frank, and becoming indispensable to the continuation of Leander's legacy. The forge, in a small but significant way, had found its new hands.

Chapter 23

Months turned into a year. The Frost forge, under Frank's steady leadership and Edwin's rapidly developing skill, continued to thrive. Edwin had not left Pondicherry, but his status as a journeyman meant he was now entrusted with more complex and independent commissions. His proficiency grew, and soon, his reputation began to extend beyond the immediate village. He was no longer just the former Town Farm boy; he was Edwin Littlefield, a skilled blacksmith, trusted and capable.

One crisp autumn morning, a commission arrived at the forge that would pull Edwin further afield than usual. It was a substantial job from North Pondicherry, from one of the newer, grand brick houses being built on the more affluent outskirts of town. The property, it turned out, belonged to Simon and Nan Libby. They needed custom ironwork for their new gates, intricate railings for a sweeping staircase, and several decorative pieces for the exterior. It was a prestigious, well-paying job, and Frank, acknowledging Edwin's growing expertise in fine work, assigned him to oversee the bulk of it.

"This is a good opportunity, Edwin," Frank had said, clapping him on the shoulder. "Show them what the Frost forge can do."

And so, for several weeks, Edwin spent his days in North Pondicherry, making trips back and forth from the main forge as needed, but often working on-site to measure, fit, and install the elaborate ironwork. The Libby residence was indeed a grand brick house, imposing and elegant, reflecting Simon's burgeoning political ambitions and the family's substantial wealth. From the outside, it was the picture of success and domestic bliss.

As Edwin worked, quietly and diligently, he became an almost invisible fixture on the periphery of their lives. He would see Nan, now Mrs. Simon Libby, moving through her grand house or supervising the garden. She looked as beautiful as ever, perhaps even more refined, perfectly embodying the role of a senator's daughter-in-law. Yet, as the weeks wore on, Edwin began to notice subtle things, cracks in the gleaming facade.

He saw Nan, sometimes, with a faint shadow under her eyes, or a stillness in her posture that belied the cheerful politeness she always extended to him. He'd observe brief, clipped conversations between her and Simon, the tension in the air almost palpable, even if the words were too low to discern. Simon, always charming in public, seemed to have a sharper edge in the privacy of his home, a quick impatience in his voice that Edwin hadn't heard before. There were moments when Nan would flinch almost imperceptibly at a sudden movement or a raised tone from Simon, quickly recovering herself with a polite smile that didn't quite reach her eyes.

He also noticed the frequent, unannounced visits of Senator Nat Libby. The Senator, still as outwardly charming as ever, would often arrive unbidden, his presence casting a long, almost possessive shadow over the household. Edwin would catch glimpses of him engaging Nan in conversation, his voice a low murmur, his hand sometimes resting a moment too long on her arm or back, a continuation of the "smarmy" attention Edwin had witnessed at that earlier dinner. Nan's responses were always polite, but Edwin sensed a growing reserve in her, a quiet retreat behind a wall of decorum.

The grand brick house, with its meticulously crafted ironwork and man-icured lawns, began to feel less like a home of happiness and more like a gilded cage. Edwin, with his quiet nature and keen observations honed by years of seeing the truth beneath surfaces at the Town Farm, could feel the subtle vibrations of discord. All, it seemed, was not well with the newlyweds, despite the outward show of a perfect society marriage. The silence often spoke louder than any words.

One afternoon, as Edwin was meticulously fitting a section of the wrought-iron railing near the side entrance, he heard a familiar, booming voice. "Well, I'll be. Edwin? Is that truly you?"

It was Senator Nat Libby. He had just stepped from his carriage, dressed immaculately, his smile broad but his eyes sharp. His expression quickly shifted from genial surprise to something far less welcoming. He recognized the boy from the Town Farm, an inconvenient link to a history he needed buried. A prickle of cold dread ran through Nat. His run for the governorship was well underway, and the merest hint of scandal, any connection to the perceived unsavory elements of the Town Farm, could be disastrous. Specifically, he worried that Edwin's very presence, his history, could lead to the uncovering of a secret long buried, a truth about Edwin's parentage that, if revealed, would utterly ruin Nat Libby. The thought that Edwin might somehow know, or accidentally discover, the truth filled him with a chilling fear.

"Senator Libby," Edwin replied, inclining his head respectfully, hammer still in hand.

Nat Libby stepped closer, his voice dropping to a low, almost conspiratorial tone, his eyes boring into Edwin's. "Still working for the Frosts, eh? A steady hand, I hear. Yes, quite. But tell me, Edwin, you've always been a... quiet observer, haven't you? Taken in a good deal, I'm sure, of all sorts of goings-on in this town." He paused, his gaze fixed on Edwin, his smile tightening. "Some things, Edwin, are best kept to oneself. Especially when one finds oneself in... elevated company. Loose lips, you understand, can cause no end of trouble. For everyone involved. Past and present." The last words were spoken with a particular emphasis, a silent question hidden within the threat. He was trying to gauge if Edwin knew anything, if the very secret he feared was stirring.

Edwin met the Senator's gaze, his own expression unreadable. He understood the implied threat, the warning woven into the smooth words. The Senator was worried about something. Edwin's presence, his quiet observations, and his past connection to the Sanborns and the Town Farm, were a direct conduit to the very secret that could ruin the powerful Libby family's ambitions, especially with Nat seeking the highest office in the state. But of the deeper, darker secret, the true source of Nat Libby's fear regarding his parentage, Edwin was completely and utterly in the dark. He simply registered the Senator's unusual intensity, adding another layer of unease to the opulent, yet strained, atmosphere of the Libby household.

The Senator's veiled warning had left an acrid taste in Edwin's mouth, but he pushed it aside, focusing on the meticulous fitting of the final sections of railing. He was almost done with the commission, and then he could return to the steadier, if less opulent, work at the Frost forge. Yet, the unease about Nan lingered, a faint discord beneath the outward harmony of the grand house.

He was working near the front entrance one late afternoon, just finishing securing one of the ornate gates, when voices, sharp and rising, drifted from inside. It was Simon and Nan, their argument escalating. Edwin paused, his tools momentarily forgotten, a knot tightening in his gut. He heard Simon's voice, cold and laced with a cutting contempt he hadn't fully recognized before. Then Nan's, strained and pleading.

Suddenly, the heavy front door burst open. Simon stood in the threshold, his face contorted with fury, his hand still extended as if he'd just shoved something. Behind him, on the polished wood floor of the entryway, Nan stumbled, crying out as she lost her footing. Simon, without hesitation, swung his arm, a sickening smack echoing in the quiet air, and then, with a brutal shove, sent her tumbling down the grand entryway staircase. Her body bounced once, twice, before she landed in a crumpled heap at the bottom, her breath knocked out of her, a strangled gasp escaping her lips.

For a moment, Edwin was frozen, the horror of the scene paralyzing him. Then, a raw, protective fury surged through him, eclipsing everything else. He dropped his tools with a clatter and sprinted towards the steps. "You bastard!" he roared, launching himself at Simon. His fist connected with Simon's jaw with a satisfying thud, a punch born of pure, incandescent rage. Simon reeled back, staggering, a look of shocked disbelief on his face as he clutched his jaw.

Edwin started down the steps towards Nan, who lay bruised and gasping, her hand already rising to her face where a dark mark was rapidly blossoming beneath her eye. "Nan, are you..."

Before he could reach her, Simon, recovered from the blow, let out a guttural cry of his own. He launched himself at Edwin, tackling him from behind. The two men tumbled, a whirlwind of fists and grunts. Simon, fueled by a narcissistic fury at being challenged and struck, fought dirty, aiming for soft spots. Edwin, though smaller, fought with the desperate strength of a man defending the helpless. The thuds of their blows mingled with Nan's frightened sobs.

Then, a shout from the side. The hired man, who tended to the horses in the barn, ran around the corner, alarmed by the commotion. He was a burly fellow, and he wasted no time. With surprising speed, he plunged between the two combatants, grabbing each by the scruff of the neck and wrenching them apart with powerful arms. "Enough! What in God's name is going on here?"

Edwin, panting, felt a warm trickle on his upper lip. He touched it, bringing his fingers away bloody. His nose was bleeding freely. He was bruised and aching, but his gaze immediately went to Nan, who was trying to push herself up, her face a mask of pain and mortification.

Seeing Edwin's bleeding nose, a flicker of true concern crossed Nan's bruised face. She scrambled up and, ignoring Simon completely, ran into the house, her voice trembling. "A towel! I'll get a towel!"

Simon, his jaw swelling, glared at Edwin with pure venom. He didn't speak, but his furious gaze promised retribution. Then, he spun on his heel and stalked off towards the barn, his steps heavy with seething rage. Moments later, the thundering of hooves erupted from the barn, and Simon wheeled out on his stallion, riding hell for leather down the drive and towards town, a dark, furious silhouette against the setting sun.

Edwin moved to Nan, who was returning with a damp cloth, her hands shaking. She looked terribly vulnerable, her face swelling, her eyes wide with humiliation. He tried to comfort her, his touch gentle as she pressed the cloth to his bleeding nose.

"Nan," Edwin said, his voice low and steady, cutting through the chaos, "has he... has he done this before?"

She flinched, pulling the towel away from his face, her gaze darting away. "Edwin, please... it's nothing, truly. Just a... a misunderstanding." Her voice was barely a whisper, thick with shame.

He caught her chin gently, turning her face so her bruised eye was starkly visible. His gaze was calm, unwavering, filled not with judgment, but with a deep, quiet concern. "Nan," he repeated, his voice softer, "Tell me the truth."

Under his steady, empathetic gaze, the dam broke. Her composure shattered, and her chin began to tremble. Tears welled in her good eye, overflowing and running down her bruised cheek. "Yes," she choked out, a raw, broken sound. "Yes, he has." She buried her face in her hands, her shoulders shaking with silent sobs. "The first time... was on our wedding night." Her voice was muffled by her hands, but the words hung heavy in the air between them, brutal and heartbreaking. She sobbed harder, the elegant setting of the grand house suddenly feeling like a cruel mockery of her reality.

Edwin knelt beside her, his own blood still slowly trickling from his nose, forgotten. A cold, hard fury began to set in, replacing the initial shock. It was a fury that resonated deep within his bones, born of the raw injustice he had witnessed so often at the Town Farm, now laid bare and personal before him. First, that a man like Simon Libby, with his polished facade and privileged existence, could harbor such a vicious, cowardly cruelty within him. But even more so, that he could treat Nan this way. Nan, with her bright spirit, her kindness, the girl who had brought a flicker of light into his own darkest days, now broken and bruised, confessing to a torment that began on the very day she was supposed to find happiness.

He wanted to hit Simon again, to keep hitting him until the handsome mask was shattered completely. But Simon was gone, and Nan was here, trembling and undone. Edwin reached out a tentative hand, resting it gently on her shaking shoulder.

"Nan," he murmured, his voice rough with emotion, "I... I am so sorry. So terribly sorry." He searched for more words, but they caught in his throat. What comfort could he offer against such a violation? He, a blacksmith, an orphan from the Farm, against the wealth and power of the Libbys. What could he possibly do?

Nan lifted her head, her swollen eye meeting his. The shame was palpable in her gaze, mingled with a desperate vulnerability. "You... you must go, Edwin," she whispered, pulling away slightly. "If Simon finds you here... if he knew I told you..." Her voice trailed off, a fresh wave of fear washing over her. "You saw. He's... he's capable of anything."

Edwin felt a surge of protectiveness so fierce it startled him. He looked at her bruised face, the black eye already deepening, and then at his own blood-stained hand. Simon Libby was a monster, hidden beneath a gentleman's veneer, and Nan was trapped. His mind raced, struggling to reconcile the public image of the rising political dynasty with the horrifying reality he had just witnessed. Senator Libby's warning echoed in his ears – "loose lips... cause no end of trouble." Now, that warning felt less about Edwin's parentage and more about the dark secrets within this very house.

"I won't leave you like this," Edwin stated, his jaw tightening. He stood, offering her his hand. Nan hesitated, then took it, letting him help her to her feet. The simple act of connection was profound. "We need to get you inside. And... and you need to tell someone. Your mother. Your father."

Nan shook her head vehemently, tears streaming anew. "No! Oh, Edwin, you don't understand. It would ruin everything. My mother... she's so proud. And Simon's father... his campaign. They'd never believe me. They'd say I was hysterical, or worse." The thought of exposing this truth, of shattering the carefully constructed image of her marriage, seemed as terrifying to her as Simon's brutality.

Edwin looked around the grand, silent exterior of the house, the perfect facade. He knew she was right, in a way. The word of a Town Farm girl, even a seminary-educated one, against a prominent political family? The shame would fall on her.

"Just… let me help you inside," Edwin said softly, his voice firm despite his internal turmoil. He knew he couldn't force her, not yet. But he also knew he couldn't forget what he'd seen. The cracks in the Libby's gilded cage were far deeper and more insidious than he had ever imagined. And now, he was inextricably, dangerously aware of them.

Before Edwin could even get Nan fully into the house, the thundering of hooves returned, louder this time, accompanied by the clatter of a carriage. Simon was back, and he hadn't come alone. The Pondicherry Sheriff, Thaddeus Thompson, a stern-faced man with a thick mustache, rode up the drive, followed closely by Senator Nat Libby in his personal carriage, his face a mask of furious concern.

Simon dismounted his stallion with a practiced leap, striding towards them, his earlier rage replaced by a terrifying calm. He pointed directly at Edwin, his voice ringing with false righteousness. "Sheriff! Thank heavens you're here! This… this man!" He gestured wildly towards Edwin. "He attacked my wife! I was merely protecting her, and he turned on me!"

Nan, still leaning on Edwin, stiffened. Her eyes, already wide with pain and fear, flickered with fresh terror. Simon rushed to her side, his arm going solicitously around her shoulders, pulling her close. He whispered something to her, too low for Edwin to hear, but Nan flinched. He then turned her slightly, shielding her bruised eye from direct view, while subtly pressing her against him, as if she were a fragile object needing his protection.

Sheriff Thompson's gaze swept from the disheveled Edwin, whose nose was still bleeding, to the seemingly distraught Simon and the clearly distressed Nan. Nat Libby, stepping from his carriage with an air of grim authority, didn't hesitate.

"Sheriff, this is an outrage!" Senator Libby boomed, his voice carrying across the drive. "This ruffian, this… Town Farm vagrant, assaulting my son and daughter-in-law on their own property! I demand he be arrested immediately! This is an affront to everything decent!" His eyes, burning with a cold calculation, met Edwin's, a silent promise of ruin. His governorship campaign flashed in his mind; this loose end must be tied up.

Edwin stared, numb with disbelief. The blatant lie, the swift manipulation, the overwhelming power arrayed against him. He opened his mouth to speak, to refute the outrageous accusation, but Sheriff Thompson, already convinced by the Senator's authority and Simon's convincing performance, stepped forward.

"Edwin," the Sheriff said, his voice flat, "I'm afraid I'll have to take you in."

Edwin glanced at Nan. Her eyes were pleading, desperate, but she remained silent, trapped within Simon's embrace, her head slightly bowed. The words were caught in her throat, strangled by fear and shame. He saw the truth in her gaze, but no one else would.

Resistance was futile, perhaps even dangerous. He nodded slowly, dropping his bleeding hand to his side. "Yes, Sheriff."

A moment later, Edwin's hands were cuffed behind his back. The Sheriff led him to his horse, Nan's silent, anguished gaze following him until he was hoisted onto the back of the Sheriff's mount. The last thing Edwin saw as they rode away was Nan's bruised face, framed by Simon's possessive arm, and Nat Libby's satisfied, yet still subtly anxious, expression.

The ride to the jail was short and humiliating. The Pondicherry streets, usually a source of comfort, now seemed to mock him with their normalcy. He was taken to the small, uninviting lock-up on Depot Street, the iron door clanging shut behind him with a final, echoing thud. The cell was cold, smelling of stale air and despair. Edwin, the blacksmith who had finally found a home and purpose, was once again behind bars, a prisoner not of a poor farm, but of a powerful family's lies.

The heavy iron door clanged shut with a finality that echoed through the small, dank cell. Edwin stood for a moment, listening to the retreating footsteps of Sheriff Thompson fade down the corridor. Then, he turned and surveyed his new confinement. The walls were rough-hewn stone, clammy to the touch. A narrow, cot-like bench was bolted to one wall, and a single, barred window, set high, offered a sliver of the darkening sky. The air was stale, smelling of sweat and disuse.

He sank onto the hard bench, the cold pressing through his clothes. Dejection settled over him like a shroud. This was familiar territory, a crushing echo of the Town Farm. Once again, he was an outsider, stripped of his nascent stability, trapped by forces he couldn't fight. The fury that had driven him to strike Simon now drained away, leaving only a bitter emptiness. He touched his throbbing nose, still crusted with dry blood.

Simon's lie had been so quick, so absolute. And Nan... Nan hadn't spoken up. He didn't blame her, not truly. He'd seen the terror in her eyes, the palpable fear of Simon, the shame that had silenced her. He understood the immense pressure she was under, the terrible choice she'd been forced to make. Her bruised face, already showing the angry purple of a black eye, was testament enough to Simon's savagery. But understanding didn't lessen the crushing weight of his predicament.

Who would believe him? An orphan from the Town Farm, accused by Senator Nat Libby's son, on the cusp of a gubernatorial campaign. He was a nobody, a shadow, easily disposable. He had no family to vouch for him, no influential friends to speak on his behalf. The Frosts, kind as they were, were tradesmen, not powerful enough to challenge the Libbys.

A profound loneliness, sharp and cold, pierced him. All his life, he had felt this, a fundamental aloneness. He had found a semblance of belonging at the forge, a sense of purpose and a future. But now, it felt snatched away, leaving him adrift once more. The iron bars seemed to mock his hard-won freedom, reminding him that the stain of his origins, the mark of being "from the Farm," was something he could never truly escape in the eyes of some. He was a stray, easily kicked aside. The night stretched before him, long and full of despair, without a single soul he could rely on to cut through the powerful lies that had landed him here.

He must have dozed, a fitful, uncomfortable sleep, when the clanking of keys roused him. He blinked, the weak morning light filtering through the high window doing little to dispel the gloom. But it wasn't the Sheriff. Standing outside his cell, his usually jovial face etched with concern, was Haskell Kneeland.

"Edwin, good God, what have they done?" Haskell's voice was low, filled with indignation. He'd heard snippets of the story from the returning Sheriff, enough to know something felt amiss. He was not a man to stand by when an injustice seemed to be unfolding, particularly against someone he knew to be hardworking and decent.

Haskell wasted no time. He immediately began to make inquiries among the local attorneys in Pondicherry, trying to secure representation for Edwin. But one after another, they politely, regretfully, declined. The reason, though unspoken, was clear: the name Libby carried too much weight. Senator Nat Libby's influence permeated every corner of the town, especially with his gubernatorial campaign in full swing. No one wanted to risk offending a man who could easily make or break a career. The fear was palpable.

Frustrated but undeterred, Haskell cast his net wider. He sent telegrams and made discreet inquiries, finally connecting with a lawyer from Windham, Daniel Chute. Chute was known to be a sharp, fearless attorney, less beholden to the political machinations of Pondicherry. Haskell explained the situation in grim detail – the accusation, Edwin's background, the overwhelming power of the Libby family. Chute listened, asked pointed questions, and after a short deliberation, agreed to take the case. The challenge, the sheer audacity of it, seemed to appeal to him.

Back in his cell, a spark of hope, faint but undeniable, ignited within Edwin when Haskell returned, his eyes now holding a determined light. "Edwin, I've found someone. A lawyer from Windham, Daniel Chute. He's agreed to represent you."

Edwin stared, the words taking a moment to fully register. A lawyer. Someone to fight for him. The relief was immense, almost dizzying. Yet, as the initial flood of gratitude washed over him, a colder understanding settled in. The fact that a lawyer had to be brought in from outside Pondicherry, that no one local would touch the case, spoke volumes about the formidable reach of the Libbys. He was grateful to Haskell, more than words could say, but he also understood the uneven playing field he was on.

Meanwhile, back at the grand brick house, Nan endured a night of silent torment. Simon had returned late, his anger a cold, simmering presence. He hadn't touched her, but his disdain had been a palpable thing, worse, almost, than the physical blows. She had seen Edwin taken away, knew he was suffering because of her silence, because of Simon's lie. Her bruised eye throbbed, a constant, physical reminder of the truth. Guilt, shame, and a terrifying sense of helplessness warred within her. She was Mrs. Simon Libby now, trapped in a gilded cage built by fear, with no clear path to escape, and a good man languishing in a jail cell because of her.

Chapter 24

The Pondicherry courtroom, usually reserved for mundane disputes over property lines and minor infractions, hummed with an unusual tension. The room was not large, with rows of hard wooden benches facing a raised dais where the Honorable William J. Foster, a man whose stern countenance matched the heavy oak of his bench, presided. Today, the air was thick with whispered expectation, for the case before the court touched the very top of Pondicherry society.

At the defendant's table, Edwin sat, his posture rigid despite the shackles that bound his wrists and ankles. The metallic glint of the chains was a stark contrast to the rough fabric of his clothes. His face was drawn, a pallor from sleepless nights and the raw injustice of his situation. The bridge of his nose, where Simon had struck him, was still visibly bruised, a dark, angry smear that no amount of washing could erase. His eye, too, carried a faint discoloration from the struggle. He looked, to most observers, exactly what a man accused of violence might look like – tired, battered, perhaps guilty.

Across the room, at a more comfortable table, sat Simon Libby, impeccably dressed, his jaw still slightly swollen, but otherwise unblemished. Beside him, radiating an aura of controlled indignation, was Senator Nat Libby. They exuded an air of injured innocence, a powerful family wronged.

In the first few rows of benches, Edwin could see the faces of those who had come for him. Mr. Haskell Kneeland sat closest, his brow furrowed with concern, his attention fixed on Edwin with an encouraging, if grim, expression. Behind him was Frank Frost, his customary stoicism replaced by a quiet, simmering anger, his loyalty to Edwin evident in his rigid posture.

And next to Frank, Amos Sanborn, Nan's father, a man whose plain farmer's clothes seemed out of place in this room of suits and dresses, but whose presence was steady, his gaze shrewd and watchful.

But it was in the back rows that the true heartbreak of the day resided. Nan Sanborn Libby sat quietly, almost shrinking into herself, her shoulders hunched. Her face was pale, drawn, and her left eye was a stark, angry black, a violent splash of purple and blue against the delicate skin of her cheek. It was a brutal, undeniable testament to the violence she had endured, a silent scream in the hushed courtroom. Her gaze was fixed on Edwin, a profound sorrow in their depth.

Next to her, her mother, Dorcas Sanborn, sat rigid with a fierce, protective maternal instinct. Her hand rested firmly on Nan's arm, her fingers tightening periodically. "You will not go back to that house, Nan," Dorcas whispered, her voice low but unwavering, audible only to her daughter. "You're coming home with me. You belong with your own." Nan shook her head almost imperceptibly, her lips pressed together, refusing to meet her mother's desperate gaze. "No, Mother," she murmured back, her voice thin and reedy. "I am married. My place is with my husband." The words were a recitation, a desperate attempt to cling to the societal expectations that now bound her, even as they choked her.

In the row directly behind them, a shadowy figure sat, an older woman shrouded in a dark, worn shawl pulled low over her head. Her face was mostly obscured, but a pair of keen, ancient eyes watched the proceedings with an unnerving intensity. This was Marylou Hutchins, a woman whose life had long been intertwined with the quiet tragedies and unspoken histories of Pondicherry's most vulnerable.

Judge Foster rapped his gavel, and the low murmur in the courtroom ceased. "Order! Let the proceedings begin."

The clerk read the charges: assault and battery. Sheriff Thompson then recounted Simon Libby's version of events, a carefully constructed narrative of Edwin as the aggressor. Then, Simon Libby himself took the stand, his voice clear and resonant, a practiced politician-in-the-making. He painted a picture of a crazed Edwin, inexplicably lashing out at his innocent wife, forcing Simon to intervene in her defense.

Then, to the surprise of some but not all, Senator Nat Libby rose from his seat beside his son and addressed the court. "Your Honor, if I may. As a duly licensed attorney in this state, and given the nature of the charges involving my family, I will personally represent my son in this matter." He spoke with an air of gravitas, his presence filling the small courtroom, turning a legal proceeding into a personal and political declaration. Judge Foster, after a moment's consideration, nodded his assent.

Nat Libby began his direct examination of Simon, guiding him through a narrative of unprovoked assault, of a heroic defense of his beloved wife. Simon, emboldened by his father's presence and the lack of challenge, embellished details, painting Edwin as a dangerous, unpredictable brute.

Finally, it was Daniel Chute's turn. He rose, a figure of quiet but undeniable authority, contrasting sharply with Nat Libby's theatrical pronouncements. He walked slowly to the stand, his gaze piercing as he faced Simon.

"Mr. Libby," Chute began, his voice calm, cutting through the lingering echoes of Simon's testimony. "You stated that the defendant, Mr. Littlefield, violently attacked your wife, Mrs. Libby. Is that correct?"

"He did!" Simon asserted, puffing out his chest. "A heinous, unprovoked assault!"

"And you, Mr. Libby, bravely intervened to protect her?" Chute's tone was neutral, almost bland.

"Naturally! As any husband would!" Simon's eyes darted to the gallery, playing to the spectators.

"Indeed," Chute conceded, then paused. His gaze drifted subtly towards the back of the courtroom, towards Nan. "Mr. Libby, your wife is present today. We can all observe her, clearly visible from this stand." His eyes returned to Simon, sharp and unwavering. "Can you explain to the court, then, how Mrs. Libby came to sustain the rather prominent black eye we see on her face today, given that you were supposedly protecting her from Mr. Littlefield?"

A ripple went through the courtroom. Simon blanched, his confident demeanor faltering for a split second. Nat Libby shot to his feet, his booming voice cutting across the silence. "Objection, Your Honor! Irrelevant! Counsel is attempting to malign my son's character with baseless innuendo! My son's testimony concerned the defendant's assault on Mrs. Libby, not an unrelated injury!"

Judge Foster, his expression unreadable, held up a hand. "Mr. Chute, please confine your questioning to the matter at hand. The origin of Mrs. Libby's injury, while unfortunate, is not directly before this court."

"Your Honor," Chute countered, his voice rising slightly but still controlled, "my question goes directly to the credibility of the witness's account of events. Mr. Libby claims to have been defending his wife. If the injury to Mrs. Libby's person occurred during or as a result of the very altercation he describes, then its origin is highly relevant to understanding the true nature of what transpired." He gestured towards Nan, almost imperceptibly. "Surely the court wishes to understand all the facts related to the physical state of those involved in this alleged assault?"

Nat Libby bristled, his face tightening, a vein throbbing in his temple. He knew this line of questioning was dangerous, pointing directly to the very truth he sought to bury. He met Chute's unwavering stare, recognizing the steel beneath the quiet demeanor. The battle had truly begun.

Judge Foster leaned forward, his gaze moving between the two attorneys, weighing the arguments. A palpable tension filled the courtroom, every breath held. After a moment that stretched into an eternity, he finally spoke. "The objection is overruled. Mr. Chute's line of questioning, pertaining to the physical state of those involved in the alleged incident, is relevant to assessing the credibility of the witness's testimony regarding the sequence of events. Mr. Libby, you will answer the question."

A collective gasp, quickly stifled, went through the gallery. Nat Libby's jaw clenched, but he resumed his seat, his eyes never leaving Daniel Chute, a silent promise of future reprisal.

Simon, visibly unsettled, shifted in the witness stand. He glanced nervously at Nan in the back, then quickly away, his eyes settling on his father, who gave him a subtle, almost imperceptible nod. He cleared his throat.

"Mrs. Libby's... injury," Simon began, his voice regaining some of its smooth cadence, though a faint tremor was discernible, "was, regrettably, an unfortunate accident. During the defendant's unprovoked attack on her, he... he swung wildly. My wife, in her distress, stumbled. She... she fell against a piece of furniture on the porch. It was a terrible mishap, caused by Mr. Littlefield's aggression, I assure you." He managed a look of profound regret, a performance that would have been convincing to anyone who hadn't seen the reality unfold.

Chute's lips thinned almost imperceptibly, but he pressed on. "So, Mr. Libby, you claim Mr. Littlefield, while assaulting your wife, somehow caused her to stumble against furniture, resulting in a black eye. Yet, your sworn testimony states you intervened to protect her. Are you suggesting you were unable to prevent this 'accident' despite being present and actively defending her?"

Nat Libby was on his feet again. "Objection! Argumentative! Counsel is badgering the witness!"

"Sustained," Judge Foster ruled, though his gaze lingered on Simon with a flicker of something unreadable. Chute had made his point, subtle as it was, forcing Simon to contort his story even further.

All eyes, however, had momentarily flickered to Nan as Simon spoke of her injury. When he lied about her "stumbling," a flush crept up her pale neck, and her head dropped slightly. She pressed her lips together, her already bruised eye seeming to throb even more acutely. She clutched her mother's hand beneath the shawl, her grip desperate. Dorcas, sensing her daughter's anguish, simply squeezed back, her face a mask of stone. Nan remained silent, a silent, unwilling accomplice to the lie, bound by fear and the crushing weight of her new status.

In the row behind them, Marylou Hutchins, the woman in the shawl, watched every exchange with an intensity that missed nothing. Her aged eyes, sharp as a hawk's, moved from Simon's lying face to Nat Libby's furious one, then to Nan's bowed head, and finally rested on Edwin, shackled and vulnerable. A knowing sadness filled her gaze, a profound understanding of the tangled lies and hidden truths in that courtroom.

"Your Honor," Daniel Chute continued, "I request that the court call the stable hand, Mr. Jedediah Clarke, who was present at the scene and witnessed the latter portion of the altercation, to testify."

Judge Foster nodded. "Call Mr. Jedediah Clarke to the stand."

A moment later, Jedediah Clarke, a burly man with rough, calloused hands, shuffled towards the witness stand. He looked nervous, his eyes darting around the courtroom as if searching for an escape. As he passed the Libby table, Nat Libby caught his eye, a fleeting, almost imperceptible narrowing of the Senator's eyes that Jedediah clearly understood. It was a silent, chilling reminder of the conversation they'd likely had, the unspoken threats, the promise of ruin if he deviated from the script.

Jedediah took the oath, his voice a low mumble. Daniel Chute approached him, his demeanor patient.

"Mr. Clarke," Chute began kindly, "you were at the Libby residence on the day of this incident, were you not?"

"Yes, sir. Workin' in the barn."

"And did you hear or witness anything unusual that afternoon?"

Jedediah shifted, picking at a thread on his trousers. "Heard a commotion, sir. Sounded like... hollering. Went to see what was what."

"And what did you see, Mr. Clarke, when you arrived on the scene?"

Jedediah cleared his throat, his gaze carefully avoiding Edwin Littlefield's. "Saw Mr. Libby and Mr. Littlefield, here, tangled up. They was... they was grappling. Mrs. Libby was nearby, upset. I stepped in and broke 'em apart, like."

"Did you see who initiated the physical contact?" Chute pressed, his voice gentle but insistent.

Jedediah hesitated. His eyes flickered towards Nat Libby, who was watching him with an unnerving intensity. "Well, sir, it was all of a sudden, you see. Bit of a blur. Just saw 'em going at it."

"You did not see Mr. Littlefield strike Mrs. Libby, as Mr. Simon Libby has testified?" Chute asked directly, leaning slightly forward.

Jedediah swallowed hard. "Didn't rightly see that, no, sir. Just saw 'em grappling. Mrs. Libby, she was real upset, like I said." He emphasized "upset," trying to sound helpful without explicitly contradicting Simon.

"And did you observe Mrs. Libby's condition?"

"She was distressed, yes, sir." Jedediah's eyes flickered to Nan, then away. "Her face was... she was upset." He avoided mentioning the bruise, focusing on the general distress.

Chute persisted, trying to lead him. "Was there any visible injury to Mrs. Libby's face?"

Nat Libby rose, not even bothering to object, simply fixing Jedediah with a stare. Jedediah seemed to shrink. "Couldn't rightly say, sir. Just saw she was distraught. My concern was breaking up the fight." His voice was barely above a whisper, carefully crafted to avoid blame or truth.

Chute sighed, a silent frustration. It was clear Jedediah Clarke had been thoroughly intimidated, a puppet on the Libby's strings. He knew he wouldn't get the full truth from him. "No further questions for this witness, Your Honor."

The testimony, while not outright damning for Edwin, certainly hadn't helped him. It confirmed a fight, but conveniently obscured the crucial details of its initiation and the cause of Nan's injury. It reinforced the narrative that Edwin Littlefield was violent and volatile, while Simon remained the aggrieved party.

Edwin Littlefield watched Jedediah shuffle back to his seat, a cold knot tightening in his stomach. The system was rigged. The power of the Libby name was a suffocating blanket, smothering the truth. He felt the familiar despair creep back in, the echo of the Town Farm. He was truly alone, facing an unassailable wall of influence. He looked to Haskell, whose face was grim, and Frank, whose anger was now a quiet, dangerous fire in his eyes.

In the back, Nan's head remained bowed, her secret safe but her heart heavy. She knew the truth, and the burden of it was immense. Marylou, however, watched the proceedings with renewed intensity. Jedediah's carefully evasive testimony, the blatant intimidation, solidified something within her. The Libbys thought they were untouchable. But Marylou knew a truth that could bring their entire edifice crashing down. The appropriate time, she mused, was drawing very, very near.

Daniel Chute, however, refused to be deterred. He knew the Libbys had successfully neutralized Jedediah. Now, he would pivot. He needed to build a positive case for Edwin, one based on character, and find a way to undermine Simon's claims more directly.

"Your Honor," Chute announced, his voice ringing with renewed purpose, "the defense calls Mr. Frank Frost to the stand."

Frank Frost, tall and broad-shouldered, moved with a quiet dignity to the witness box. He took the oath solemnly, his gaze briefly meeting Edwin's, a silent message of solidarity passing between them.

Chute began. "Mr. Frost, you are the owner of the Frost Forge, are you not?"

"That's right, sir."

"And Mr. Edwin Littlefield has been your apprentice, and now your journeyman, for some time?"

"Yes, since my father hired him on." Frank nodded, his eyes going soft for a moment at the mention of Leander. "He's a good hand, and a good man."

"Mr. Frost," Chute continued, "in all the time Mr. Littlefield has lived and worked under your roof, have you ever known him to be a man of violence? Have you ever witnessed him to have a 'savage temper,' as Mr. Simon Libby has claimed?"

"Never," Frank stated, his voice firm and unwavering. "Edwin's a quiet man. Hardworking. He minds his own business. I've never seen him raise a hand in anger, not once. He's got a steady hand at the anvil, not a wild one."

Nat Libby rose for cross-examination, his tone dripping with condescension. "Mr. Frost, you're merely a blacksmith, are you not? Not a man of letters, or of law. How would you presume to understand the complexities of a man's hidden temper, especially one from... the unfortunate circumstances of the Town Farm?"

Frank's jaw tightened, but he held his ground. "I know the measure of a man by his work and his word, Senator. And by that measure, Edwin's a better man than many who wear fine suits."

"Indeed," Nat sneered, turning his back on Frank as if dismissing him. "No further questions." He seemed confident that he had undermined Frank's testimony by belittling his profession and Edwin's origins.

As Frank returned to his seat, Chute glanced at Edwin, then at Nan. He knew he had to address the bruise more directly, more convincingly. He decided on a bold move.

"Your Honor," Chute stated, turning to the bench, "I would like to recall Mr. Simon Libby to the stand for further cross-examination."

A stir went through the courtroom. Nat Libby's face darkened, but the Judge, intrigued, allowed it. Simon, looking annoyed, reluctantly returned to the witness stand.

"Mr. Libby," Chute began, his voice taking on a sharper edge. "You have testified that Mrs. Libby sustained her injury by 'stumbling against furniture' during Mr. Littlefield's 'wild flailing.' Is that still your testimony?"

"It is," Simon affirmed, though a hint of defiance crept into his tone.

"Mr. Libby," Chute leaned forward, his voice dropping, "do you, by chance, wear a ring on your right hand?"

Simon's eyes flickered, surprised. He instinctively looked down at his right hand, where a heavy signet ring, bearing the Libby crest, gleamed. "I... I do. It's a family heirloom."

"And you wear it regularly?"

"Yes."

"Mr. Libby," Chute continued, his voice rising now, "Mrs. Libby's injury, that prominent black eye, has a distinct, circular mark at its center. A mark, I would suggest, consistent with the impact of a blunt object, perhaps even, a heavy ring. Could it be, Mr. Libby, that the 'furniture' Mrs. Libby 'stumbled' against was, in fact, your hand? Your hand, wearing that very ring?"

A gasp went through the courtroom. Nat Libby was on his feet, roaring, "Objection! Outrageous! Your Honor, counsel is making an unsubstantiated accusation of spousal abuse! This is scurrilous!"

"Your Honor," Chute thundered, his voice cutting through the objection, "the witness's credibility is paramount! His explanation for his wife's injuries is demonstrably weak when faced with the physical evidence! A black eye from a fall against furniture? Or from a fist, adorned with a ring, in a fit of temper?"

Judge Foster rapped his gavel repeatedly, his face flushed. "Order! Order in the court! Mr. Chute, you are treading on very thin ice! I will allow the question, but I warn you against direct accusations without further evidence."

Simon, his face now a mask of fury and fear, opened his mouth to deny, to bluster, but he suddenly caught Nat Libby's eye. His father's gaze was not one of outrage, but of utter, cold panic. The word "spousal abuse" hung in the air, a venomous, political death knell. Nat knew that if this accusation, however unsubstantiated in court, gained any traction, his gubernatorial campaign was finished. And for a fleeting moment, as Simon saw that raw fear in his father's eyes, he saw not just the campaign, but the entire, fragile edifice of their public life threatened.

It was in that moment, as Simon struggled to compose himself and Nat Libby's face twisted with barely contained desperation, that the woman in the back row, Marylou Hutchins, made her decision. She had watched Simon's lies, seen Jedediah's fear, and felt the chilling power of Nat Libby's influence. But it was Nat's raw, animal fear, the naked vulnerability in his eyes at the mere whisper of "abuse" threatening his political dreams, combined with his continued condescension towards Edwin Littlefield, the "Town Farm vagrant" with "no family," that finally pushed her. This was the moment. The time had come for the truth, however devastating, to finally see the light. She began to rise slowly from her seat, her old shawl slipping back to reveal her weathered, determined face.

The judge had just gaveled, threatening to hold the Senator in contempt if another outburst occurred. Simon, pale and sweating, stood silent on the witness stand, caught in the harsh glare of the accusation. A tense quiet had descended on the room.

It was into this fragile silence that the woman's voice cut, surprisingly strong and clear, though raspy with age. "Your Honor! Ladies and gentlemen of the court!"

Every head snapped towards the back row. All eyes, including the Judge's, were now fixed on the old woman who stood there, her shawl fallen to her shoulders, revealing a face etched with decades of hardship and secret-keeping, now radiating an undeniable, furious resolve.

Nat Libby froze. His eyes, already wide with a different kind of panic, widened further still as he recognized her. A wave of sick dread washed over him, draining the color from his face. He knew her. He knew what she knew. His lips parted, but no sound came out, as if his throat had seized.

The judge banged his gavel. "Order! Order! What is your name, Madam?"

"My name is Marylou Hutchins. This is not just about what this Libby boy did to his wife yesterday," she declared, her voice growing in power, sweeping over the hushed courtroom. She pointed a trembling, accusatory finger directly at Simon. "And it's not just about what he just said about Edwin Littlefield here!" Her finger then swung dramatically towards Nat Libby, who was now visibly trembling, a sheen of sweat breaking out on his forehead. "It's about the Libby men, and the way they treat women, and the secrets they bury to protect their precious names!"

A collective gasp rippled through the courtroom, quickly followed by a chaotic murmur. Judge Foster pounded his gavel. "Order! Order! Madam, you are out of order! State your business or you will be removed!"

Marylou ignored him. Her gaze, fierce and unyielding, was locked on Nat Libby. "This man," she cried, pointing directly at the Senator, "he forced himself on Hannah Littlefield! Edwin's mother! When she was barely more than a girl!"

The courtroom erupted. Whispers turned into shouts. Judge Foster hammered his gavel with desperate force, his face red. Haskell Kneeland shot upright, his mouth agape. Frank Frost clenched his fists, a stunned, horrified realization dawning on his face. Amos Sanborn, though perhaps sensing some of it before, now watched in stark disbelief.

Marylou pressed on, her voice raw with years of suppressed truth. "Hannah's father, he was a proud, foolish man. He threw her out, wouldn't have her shame his name! But her mother, bless her soul, she loved her girl. She sent Hannah to her aunt's house, far away, to hide her shame. But they found out. They found out Hannah was pregnant. And they knew they had to protect her, and that baby, from the likes of Nat Libby!"

She paused, her breath coming in ragged gasps, but her eyes never left Nat, who sat slumped, utterly defeated, his political career crumbling around him with every word.

"They couldn't let Nat Libby touch that child, corrupt it, deny it," Marylou continued, her voice heavy with grief. "So they came to me. An old family friend. They secreted her at the Town Farm, in my care. She was hidden there, away from prying eyes, away from his reach." Her finger jabbed towards Nat again. "But it wasn't enough. The shame, the hardship.... Hannah died in childbirth, Your Honor! She died, leaving behind this boy, Edwin!" Her arm swept towards Edwin, who sat in stunned silence, his face ghostly pale, staring at Marylou as if she had just materialized from thin air. His own origins, his entire life's mystery, was being laid bare in the most public and devastating way imaginable.

"Nat Libby suspected," Marylou went on, oblivious to the pandemonium. "He suspected this Littlefield boy was his, but he wasn't sure! He sent his men, poked around, tried to find proof, tried to find Hannah's baby! He tried to isolate the boy, keep anyone from finding out the truth! He didn't want any stain on his precious name, not with his ambitions! But I knew! I knew it all! And I swore to the babe's mother I'd protect her boy, even from his own father!"

She turned her gaze from Nat to Simon, her voice laced with bitter condemnation. "And what do we see now? The son, acting just like the father! Hurting women, lying about it, trying to use influence and power to bury the truth! The apple doesn't fall far from the tree, does it? A Libby man, treating a woman like she's nothing but property, fit to be abused and then silenced!"

The courtroom had descended into utter chaos. Shouts of "Scandal!" and "Disgrace!" erupted from the gallery. Reporters scribbled furiously. Judge Foster was pounding his gavel so hard it seemed it might splinter, his face a mixture of shock and fury.

Nat Libby sagged in his seat, his head bowed, utterly broken. His gubernatorial dreams, his carefully constructed reputation, his entire life's work, were shattering around him. He made no attempt to silence Marylou, his eyes fixed on the floor, the horrifying truth undeniable.

Simon Libby stared at his father, then at Edwin, then at Marylou, his face a mask of disbelief. The implications were staggering, horrifying. He, the perfect scion of the perfect family, suddenly tied to such a monstrous secret, to a man he now realized was his half-brother, conceived in violence.

Edwin Littlefield sat frozen, the shackles on his limbs forgotten. His mind reeled. His mother. Hannah Littlefield. Dead in childbirth. His father... Nat Libby? The man who had imprisoned him, whose son had abused Nan, whose family had treated him like dirt. His entire identity, his past, present, and future, had just been irrevocably, violently rewritten.

Nan, beside her mother, gasped, her bruised eye wide with horror, not just for herself, but for the profound, terrible truth she had just witnessed unfold. Her own abuse suddenly connected to a deeper, generational pattern of malevolent power. Her mother, Dorcas, held her tighter, her own eyes blazing, now filled with a righteous fury. The silent suffering of generations of women, now brought to light by one brave, old woman.

The entire courtroom was in an uproar, the scales of justice suddenly tipped, not by legal argument, but by the raw, undeniable weight of a long-buried truth. A murmur, low and uncertain at first, rippled through the gallery, quickly swelling into a shocked clamor. Eyes, wide with dawning horror and disbelief, darted from the now-pale Senator Libby to Edwin.

It wasn't just the assault, the violation of a young girl, or even the implication of arson that ignited the crowd. It was something far more than that now, something that dug into the very pockets of every working man and woman in Pondicherry. Someone in the back, Andrew Kimball, a farmer whose relentless hard work barely kept his own family afloat, mumbled just loud enough for others to hear, "The Town Farm..."

The words hung in the air, a poisonous bloom. Then another voice, sharper, picked it up, "The poor farm! They sent her to the poor farm!"

And then, the horrible, undeniable sum began to form in their minds.

The feed for the animals. The wages for Marylou, for the Superintendents. The coal for the stoves, the candles for the long nights. The cost of the new barn. The thread for Edwin's patched overalls, the very bread he ate.

Every expense, every meager penny contributed to the upkeep of the Town Farm, had, for all those years, gone towards raising his child. Nat Libby's bastard. The child of the man who lived in the grandest house, who held the most sway, who controlled the very bank that held their savings. The same man who, in his arrogance and power, had ensured Hannah Littlefield, the mother, was cast out, forcing the town to shoulder the burden of his sin.

A collective gasp, a hiss of fury, swept through the room. Faces twisted from shock to indignation, then to outright rage. Fingers, gnarled from labor, curled into fists. The sense of betrayal was palpable, thick and suffocating. It wasn't just a moral failing; it was a profound, personal swindle. They, the honest, hardworking folk of Pondicherry, had been played for fools, forced to pay for the secret sins of their richest citizen.

The judge hammered his gavel, the sound lost in the rising tide of outrage. This wasn't just a legal trial anymore. This was the reckoning of a town scorned.

Chapter 25

The Pondicherry courtroom was a maelstrom. Marylou's words, sharp and devastating, hung in the air, each syllable a hammer blow against the polished facade of the Libby name. Nat Libby, finally finding his voice, erupted. He sprang to his feet, overturning his chair with a crash, his face contorted with a mixture of rage and terror.

"Your Honor! What is the meaning of this outrage?!" he bellowed, his voice raw and uncontrolled, echoing off the wooden walls. "Do your job! Silence this... this madwoman! This is a court of law, not a public circus for baseless slander!" He pointed a shaking finger at Marylou. "You would take the word of a mere servant, a common Town Farm attendant, against mine? This woman is lying! She has no proof! This is a conspiracy!"

Judge Foster, his face ashen but his will firm, pounded his gavel with furious, relentless force. "Order! Order in this court! Mr. Libby, control yourself, or I will hold you in contempt! Sheriff, clear the room if order cannot be restored!"

Slowly, painfully, a semblance of calm was regained, though the air still crackled with electric tension. Spectators whispered frantically, their eyes darting between the disgraced Senator, the defiant old woman, and the shackled Edwin Littlefield.

When the furious murmuring subsided to a tense hum, Nat Libby, visibly struggling to regain his composure, straightened his suit. His eyes, though still wild with fear, now held a cold, calculating glint. He addressed the court, his voice regaining some of its familiar oratorical power, though laced with a desperate edge. "Your Honor, ladies and gentlemen, this is a clear attempt to discredit a respected family, a political figure, with malicious falsehoods. This woman, Mrs. Hutchins, offers no proof! She offers nothing but the ramblings of a deranged mind, a mere servant whose word counts for nothing against the reputation of honorable men!" He gestured dismissively at Marylou. "This is an absurd diversion, a libelous accusation meant to sway this court from the actual charges!"

But before Nat Libby could fully launch into his counter-offensive, a quiet but firm voice cut across his, echoing Marylou's earlier defiance. From the row directly in front of Marylou, an older woman, dressed simply but with an air of quiet dignity, slowly stood up. She looked directly at Judge Foster, her gaze calm and steady.

"My name is Rebecca Lewis," she stated, her voice clear and resonant, carrying to every corner of the room. She was known to many in Pondicherry; a respected member of the church community, involved in various charities and always taking an interest in the less fortunate. Her reputation was unimpeachable. "Mrs. Hutchins speaks the truth."

A fresh wave of murmurs rippled through the courtroom, louder this time. Nat Libby's face crumpled further, a gasp escaping his lips. His head snapped towards Rebecca Lewis, his eyes wide with a new, horrifying realization.

Rebecca Lewis ignored him. Her gaze, filled with a deep sorrow and an even deeper resolve, swept from Marylou to Edwin Littlefield. "It was I who took Hannah Littlefield to the Town Farm to keep her safe," she declared, her voice ringing with conviction. "Her mother, my own sister, sent her to me to keep her safe from him." Her arm, steady, lifted and pointed directly at Nat Libby, now a grotesque parody of his former self. "And I protected her at all costs from this vile and violent man!"

Edwin Littlefield's head snapped up. He stared at Mrs. Lewis, the church lady who had always given him a kind word, who had occasionally brought books to the Town Farm, who had quietly supported his efforts at education and shown an uncanny, almost maternal, interest in his welfare. He had always seen her as a benevolent figure, but now, a profound, dizzying wonder filled his mind. This was Mrs. Lewis... his grandaunt? He had family? All these years of being an orphan, of believing himself utterly alone in the world, and suddenly, shockingly, there were people in this very room who were his.

People who had known his mother, who had protected her, who had protected him. The revelation hit him with a force that far eclipsed the physical blows he had endured, washing over him with a mixture of overwhelming relief and staggering disbelief.

In the face of Mrs. Lewis's unflinching testimony, the court again erupted, this time with a furious, indignant roar. People shouted, some stood, aghast at the depth of the scandal. Judge Foster's gavel became a frantic drumbeat against the escalating chaos.

Amidst the uproar, a voice from the gallery, rough and defiant, sliced through the din. "What about the Littlefields?!" a man named Mr. Johnson shouted, standing abruptly in his seat. "They died in that fire five years ago! The whole family gone! I allus thought it was awful suspicious!"

The new accusation hung in the air, a chilling, terrifying echo to the already exposed truths, plunging the courtroom into an even deeper abyss of shock and dark suspicion. The implications of murder, of a deliberate act to erase the evidence, now loomed over the already shattered Libby family.

The courtroom's frenzy reached a fever pitch. Judge Foster, his face pale, pounded his gavel repeatedly, the sound almost swallowed by the clamor. He pointed furiously at the Sheriff. "Clear the court! Clear the court immediately! Any further outburst, and I will hold everyone in contempt!"

It took several tense minutes for the Sheriff and his deputies to restore a semblance of order, ushering out most of the stunned spectators, leaving only the key players and a handful of intrepid reporters. The air, though quieter, was thick with the weight of the accusations.

Seizing the moment, Daniel Chute stepped forward, his face grim but resolute. "Your Honor," he stated, his voice resonating with newfound authority, "given the extraordinary and highly credible revelations that have come to light regarding the true identity of the defendant, Mr. Edwin Littlefield, and the deeply disturbing allegations concerning the plaintiff's family and the circumstances surrounding Mr. Littlefield's birth and his mother's death – allegations which directly undermine the credibility of the entire Libby testimony – I move for the immediate dismissal of all charges against Mr. Edwin Littlefield."

He paused, letting the weight of his words settle. "Furthermore," Chute continued, his gaze sweeping to Simon, then to Nat Libby, "I ask that this court consider the immediate arrest of Mr. Simon Libby on charges of assault, not only against Mr. Littlefield, but against Mrs. Nan Libby, whose visible injuries speak volumes more than any fabricated testimony."

Nat Libby, still slumped, visibly flinched at the mention of "assault." Simon, across the room, looked like a hunted animal.

Judge Foster, his expression grave, scanned the quieted courtroom. He looked at Edwin, then at Marylou, then at Rebecca Lewis, her face resolute. The facts, suddenly and irrevocably, had changed everything. The original charge against Edwin Littlefield now seemed a cruel farce, a diversion.

"Given the highly irregular and profoundly serious nature of the testimony presented this day," Judge Foster announced, his voice firm and clear, cutting through the remaining tension, "and the severe impact these revelations have on the credibility of the prosecution's witnesses and the very foundation of the complaint before this court..." He paused, taking a deep breath. "I agree. The charges against Mr. Edwin Littlefield are hereby dismissed."

A collective, quiet gasp went through the remaining attendees. Edwin, shackled at the defendant's table, felt a tremor run through him. Dismissed. He was free.

Judge Foster then fixed his gaze on Simon Libby. "Sheriff Thompson," he commanded, his voice cold and unwavering, "you are hereby ordered to arrest Mr. Simon Libby on charges of assault and battery. And furthermore," his eyes now turned to Nat Libby, who seemed to shrink under the weight of his words, "Mr. Nat Libby, I strongly advise you to seek legal counsel immediately. This court expects a thorough and complete investigation into the serious allegations raised here today concerning your past conduct and the circumstances of Hannah Littlefield's death, and indeed, the tragic fire that claimed her parents."

The Sheriff moved towards Simon, who offered no resistance, his face pale and defeated. The perfect facade of the Libby family had shattered into a million pieces.

A deputy approached Edwin Littlefield, the sound of his jingling keys a melody of liberation. With quick, practiced movements, the heavy shackles were removed from Edwin's wrists and ankles. He rubbed his chafed skin, feeling the blessed lightness, the incredible freedom.

As he stood, a wave of familiar faces rushed towards him. Haskell Kneeland was the first, gripping his hand, his eyes shining with profound relief. "Edwin! Thank God! We knew!"

Frank Frost clapped him on the shoulder, a rare, wide grin breaking across his stern face. "You're free, lad. Let's get you home."

And then, Amos Sanborn stepped forward, his eyes, so often guarded, now filled with a deep, sorrowful understanding. He simply nodded, a silent acknowledgment of the shared, devastating truth about his daughter's marriage and Edwin's origins.

In the back, Nan, no longer bound by fear, watched Edwin, her bruised eye glistening with unshed tears. Relief warred with a new, complex understanding of the depths of the darkness she had married into, and the quiet heroism of the man who had suffered for her. Her mother, Dorcas, held her close, a fierce triumph in her gaze.

And by the wall, Marylou Hutchins stood with Rebecca Lewis, two quiet women who had finally brought a long-buried truth to light. Marylou met Edwin's gaze across the crowded room, a look of profound, weary satisfaction on her face. Her secret was out. And Edwin Littlefield, the orphan boy, was an orphan no more. His fight for freedom had revealed a fight for justice, and a family he never knew he had.

Chapter 26

The quiet order of Pondicherry was irrevocably shattered. The aftermath of the trial was a whirlwind of public scandal and private reckoning. Simon Libby was held without bail, his once-impeccable reputation shattered beyond repair. Nat Libby, his gubernatorial dreams utterly demolished, found himself facing not only a media frenzy but also the chilling prospect of a deeper investigation into Hannah Littlefield's death and the suspicious fire that had claimed her parents. The *Pondicherry Chronicle*, usually so deferential to the Libby name, now ran sensational headlines detailing Marylou and Rebecca Lewis's explosive testimonies. The Libbys, for the first time in generations, faced a public stripped bare of their carefully constructed power.

For Nan, the immediate consequence was a profound sense of liberation, even as it was tinged with the sorrow of her broken dreams and the visceral shock of her husband's true, cruel nature. She did not return to the grand brick house. Instead, she found solace and safety at her parents' farmhouse. Dorcas and Amos, their faces etched with pain and fierce love, welcomed her without question, their earlier disagreements about Simon fading into the background of a far greater betrayal.

With the unyielding support of her family, and Daniel Chute's continued legal guidance, Nan wasted no time in suing for divorce. The proceedings were swift, unencumbered by Simon's resistance, as he was consumed by his own legal battles. Given the public nature of the scandal and the undeniable evidence of abuse, the settlement was, not surprisingly, favorable to Nan: she was granted the brick mansion in North Pondicherry, the gilded cage she had desperately sought to escape. She had no desire to keep it. It was a monument to her suffering, a place she felt poisoned by, and she intended to sell it immediately, to sever all ties to that painful chapter of her life.

In the weeks that followed, a quiet, undeniable magnetism began to draw Nan and Edwin Littlefield together. Their shared past, stretching back to the cold confines of the Town Farm, had always been a bond, a silent understanding. Now, their shared ordeal – the public humiliation, the painful revelations, the fight for truth against a powerful enemy – forged an even deeper, more resonant connection. They found in each other a solace no one else could offer, two souls who understood, perhaps better than anyone else, the bitter taste of injustice and the quiet strength found in resilience.

When the time came to pack up the vast, echoing rooms of the brick mansion, Nan asked Edwin to help. It was a daunting task, filled with ghosts and painful memories, and she found solace in his quiet, steady presence. Edwin, Rebecca Lewis (now Aunt Rebecca to them both), and Nan's parents worked together through the house, carefully dismantling the remnants of a life that was never truly hers. One afternoon, as Edwin was carefully emptying a drawer in the formal dining room, his fingers brushed against something solid, hidden beneath a stack of linens. He pulled it out: an ornate wooden box, beautifully carved with delicate scrollwork. Curiosity piqued, he unlatched the small clasp and opened it. Inside, nestled on a bed of faded velvet, was a small, familiar shape. His breath hitched. It was the little carved bird he had made for her years ago, when she was leaving the Town Farm – the clumsy, heartfelt farewell.

He held the box open, extending it towards Nan, who was meticulously wrapping a fragile porcelain figurine nearby. She looked up, her gaze falling on the bird. In that instant, her face transformed, lighting up with a soft, radiant joy that chased away the mansion's lingering shadows.

"Oh, Edwin," she whispered, her voice thick with emotion, "my bird." She reached out, her fingers tracing the tiny, imperfect wings. "I have cherished this gift, all this time. You know," her voice grew softer, more intimate, "I would take it out sometimes, when I was lonely, or when I was scared. Just to remember the boy who made it for me. To remember kindness, and... and strength."

A warmth spread through Edwin's chest, touching a place he hadn't known was still aching. He reached into his own pocket, his fingers closing around a soft square of cotton. He pulled out the handkerchief she had made for him, all those years ago, with the painstakingly stitched letters E.L. His own simple gift, carefully treasured through the years, through every hardship.

Nan's eyes widened, recognizing it immediately. Her gaze dropped to his hand, then back to his face, a silent question forming. She reached out, her finger tracing the faded, irregular letters, the testament of her young hand. A sudden sob caught in her throat. "You kept it," she whispered, tears welling in her eyes. "My silly little gift... it mattered so much to you."

Tears streamed down her face, not of sorrow, but of a profound, overwhelming tenderness. She had felt so utterly unvalued, so discarded. And here was Edwin, proving her worth, proving that a small, forgotten gesture of affection had meant everything.

Edwin, his own eyes moist, felt his heart swell. The years of quiet longing, the unspoken understanding, converged in that moment. Without a word, he pulled her into an embrace, holding her close as her silent sobs shook her. It was a comfort born of shared history, mutual respect, and a love that had blossomed from the hard earth of adversity, blossoming now into something real and profound.

The brick mansion was sold, a painful memory discarded. Nan and Edwin painstakingly built their new future, piece by gentle piece. They married in a simple church service, quiet and heartfelt, with only their truest friends and the family they had both found – Frank and Mrs. Frost, Haskell and Marietta Kneeland, Amos and Dorcas Sanborn, Rebecca Lewis, and Marylou – bearing witness to their vows.

They settled near the forge, on the tranquil shores of Adams Pond, in a modest but sturdy home Edwin built with his own skilled hands, a place far removed from the cold grandeur of North Pondicherry. Here, amid the rhythms of the seasons and the comforting clang of the anvil, Edwin at last had all he had ever hoped for: a home of his own, a family to share it with, and work that not only sustained them but brought him deep satisfaction. He became a respected fixture in the community, his reputation as a master blacksmith growing, and his quiet wisdom and unwavering integrity earned him the esteem of his neighbors. He was quick to lend a hand to those in need, remembering always the kindness shown to him.

In time, Nan gave him the gift of a son, a boy with his mother's gentle eyes and his father's quiet strength. They named him Leander, after the man who had given Edwin his start. And as Edwin watched his son grow, secure and loved, he knew, with a certainty that warmed him to his core, that the orphaned Town Farm Boy had, against all odds, finally forged a life of true belonging, a home where his heart would forever reside.

Epilogue

The truth, once unleashed, spread through Pondicherry like wildfire, consuming the last vestiges of the Libby family's carefully constructed empire. The public outcry following the trial was unprecedented. Judge Foster, true to his word, had launched a relentless investigation into the allegations against Nat Libby. Under the weight of mounting evidence and the turning tide of public opinion, the truth about the Littlefield fire emerged, horrifying the town.

It was revealed that Nat Libby, in his desperation to bury his secret, had indeed paid an arsonist to set the fire that killed Hannah Littlefield's parents. He had intended to destroy any lingering connections to Hannah and her child, effectively erasing the past. The confession, extracted from a terrified accomplice, implicated Nat directly. The Town Farm's ledger books, meticulously kept by every Superintendent, also provided irrefutable proof of Nat Libby's financial machinations to conceal his responsibility to Edwin and force the town to bear the burden of his upkeep.

The subsequent trials were swift and merciless. Nat Libby, stripped of his political power and public respect, was convicted of conspiracy to commit arson and other related charges. His sentence was severe, a stark reminder that even the most powerful could not escape the long arm of the law. Simon Libby, already disgraced, was found guilty of assault and battery against both Edwin and Nan. He faced a hefty fine and a term in state prison, his dreams of political office and a life of privilege utterly extinguished.

The consequences extended beyond jail cells. The Libby fortune, built on generations of ambition and now tainted by revealed depravity, began to unravel. Faced with an onslaught of lawsuits, public boycotts, and dwindling influence, their financial empire crumbled. The grand South High Street mansion, scene of such avarice and brutality, was eventually sold at a fraction of its value, its very stones seemingly recoiling from the shame. The Libby name, once synonymous with power and prestige in Pondicherry, now evoked only scandal and revulsion.

For Edwin and Nan, life began anew, quieter and more profoundly rich than either had ever imagined. The little cottage by Adams Pond became their sanctuary, a place where Leander's antics mingled with Nan's gentle laughter and Edwin's quiet pride.

Rebecca Lewis, now openly Aunt Rebecca, became a constant, cherished presence. She often visited the cottage, her eyes twinkling as she would dandle young Leander on her knee, telling him stories of the quiet boy who became his father, and of the brave women who helped bring the truth to light. Leander, a sturdy, bright boy, grew up knowing he was deeply loved, secure in his identity and his family.

And Marylou Hutchins, the keeper of secrets and the catalyst for justice, found a new chapter of her own. With the weight of her lifelong burden lifted, and the quiet dignity she had always possessed now openly recognized, she found companionship with an honest, kind widower from a neighboring farm. They married in a modest ceremony, her weathered hands clasped gently in his, finally finding a peace she had long deserved.

Life in Pondicherry slowly adjusted. The scandal faded into cautionary tales, whispered lessons of hubris and hidden sins. But the changes ran deeper. The town, once so deferential to power, became more vigilant, its citizens empowered by the knowledge that truth, however long buried, could indeed rise to the surface.

Edwin and Nan, now respectfully known as Mr. and Mrs. Littlefield by their neighbors, became pillars of this evolving community. Edwin's forge thrived, his work honest and true, a stark contrast to the deceit that had once shadowed him. Nan, no longer defined by her past suffering, found her purpose in tending their home, raising their son, and quietly supporting her husband. Their love, forged in the crucible of adversity, proved stronger than any chain, more enduring than any lie. They had built not just a house, but a home, a true haven where trust and devotion bloomed, proving that even from the hardest ground, a life of deep happiness and belonging could finally take root.

Fact from Fiction

Town Farms have always fascinated me. Perhaps it's because I grew up poor, my family often on the thin edge between survival and want. Growing up in South Bridgton, Maine, the **Bridgton Town Farm** was a familiar landmark, often glimpsed on our childhood adventures—visiting Mrs. Farrand's barn and her goats, swimming in Foster Pond, or just riding bikes and rolling through yards with all the other South Bridgton kids of the time.

Town Farms were a microcosm of society, a place where the unfortunate were gathered under one roof. Each town was responsible for its own poor. Initially, those in need would be "bid out," their care handled by the lowest bidder. This system, however, often led to abuse and neglect. Town Farms emerged as a perceived solution to the persistent question: "What do we do with the poor?" By consolidating them in one location, perhaps some "economies of scale" could be achieved.

Yet, Town Farms seldom defrayed all their expenses. Rather than housing able-bodied individuals who could contribute to farm work, their populations often consisted primarily of the severely disabled or elderly. For the elderly who could no longer support themselves, the Town Farm was frequently their only option. The advent of Social Security in the 1940s significantly improved the lives of the elderly, providing them with means of support when they could no longer work.

The Seed of a Story: Wesley Kimball and Edwin Littlefield

Before the idea for this book truly took root, I was researching a man named **Wesley Kimball**. He caught my attention in an old *Bridgton News* article:

Friday, April 8, 1887 Bridgton News:

Haskell P. Kneeland, Superintendent of the town farm the past year, and who declined to serve another term, abdicated last Friday, and moved back to his own farm, "the Joseph Hazen place." Mr. Kneeland has given the best of satisfaction, he showing a human treatment of the poor, a model executive management of them and of the farm, and a business capacity promotive of the best interests of the town. Under his training, "Wesley," one of the incorrigibles, whose eccentricities had hitherto baffled former Superintendents, has ceased his disagreeable ebullitions, and now dresses and behaves like a civilized being. Mr. Kneeland is succeeded by Mr. Frank F. Johnson, of South Bridgton, who will endeavor to continue the good work of his predecessor. There are now six inmates on the farm.

An "ebullition" is a sudden outburst of emotion or violence. Wesley, to say the least, was a handful.

As I dug into Wesley's story, I discovered he was born in the distant town of Molunkus, Maine. His parents both died, and he ended up in Bridgton because of a family connection: Wesley Kimball was the great-grandson of Benjamin Kimball. Kimball was brought to the area that would become Bridgton to open a store on the shore of Long Lake. The reported origin story of Wesley's troubles was that his mother, while pregnant, was frightened by a bull, causing Wesley to be born "idiotic."

But while Wesley initially sparked my interest, it was the **1880 Census for Bridgton** that truly captured my imagination. The Census, and its accompanying *Schedule of Defective, Dependent, and Delinquent Classes*, drew my attention to **Edwin Littlefield**. Here, amongst the elderly, disabled, and "insane" inmates, was a thirteen-year-old boy. The reason he was at the Town Farm, according to the "Homeless Children" section of the Census report, was detailed as follows:

⬥

Edwin Littlefield:

- Father deceased: don't know
- Mother deceased: yes
- Abandoned by parents: yes
- Parents surrendered: yes
- Born in institution: 1877
- Admitted to institution: 1877
- Illegitimate: yes
- Has the origin of this child been respectable?: no

The others listed in the Census had a mix of problems: insane, idiotic, blind, deaf, paralysis, ulcers, old age, crippled, epilepsy. And then there was Edwin. He was at the Town Farm through no fault or deficiency of his own. I found myself wondering what stories that boy would have to tell, living side by side with all that troubled humanity. That question ultimately led to this book.

What's Real, What's Imagined: Separating Fact from Fiction
   So, what parts of *Town Farm Boy* are real, and what is fiction?

Edwin Littlefield: As noted, Edwin Littlefield was a real person listed in the 1880 Census. He conveniently disappears from historical records after this, allowing me to create a fictional story with him as the lead character.

The Superintendents: Amos Sanborn and **Haskell Kneeland** were indeed real Superintendents of the Bridgton Town Farm (and other Town Farms in the area). Because they were so well-respected, I chose to keep their names. Aside from actual reports from the *Bridgton News*, their characters and the dates of their service are used fictitiously, altered as needed for the narrative.

The other Superintendents are entirely fictional.

The Inmates: Yes, "inmates" is what the residents of Town Farms were officially called.

- **Edwin Lakin (Ned):** Edwin Lakin was a real person. In 1880, he was living at the Town Farm, listed as "maimed, crippled, or bedridden." In 1870, he lived with his father and stepmother and attended school. By 1900, the Census shows him as a farm laborer in Norway, Maine. While something clearly happened to him that led him to the Town Farm, I invented the specific story of his injury and recovery.
- **Wesley Kimball:** Wesley Kimball appears as himself. Aside from the stories of him from the *Bridgton News* (including his running away from the Farm, and being found unharmed on the shore of Peabody Pond), his character and plotlines are fictionalized. I found his "incorrigible" nature endearing (from afar.)
- **Other Inmates:** The other inmates in the story are fictional, drawn from an amalgamation of the actual residents listed in the 1880 Census and other anecdotes from local Town Farms. **Harriet Woodbury's** tragic story, for example, is entirely fictional. However, the practice of transferring inmates from the Maine Insane Hospital to Town Farms was a real cost-saving measure for towns. Two of Bridgton Town Farm's inmates in the 1880 Census had indeed previously been at the hospital, one for 15 years suffering from "melancholia," the other for 10 years suffering from "mania."

Marylou Hutchins: In the 1880 Census, a servant named Marsylvia Hutchins is listed as living and working at the Town Farm. She was a relative of Mrs. Sanborn's family. The Census taker referred to her as "Marylou," and I borrowed that name for my character. The real Mrs. Hutchins left the farm with the Sanborns and later remarried. The rest of her story in this novel, however, is purely fictional.

Leander Frost, his wife Irene, and son Frank: All three are real people. Leander and Frank were both blacksmiths. The story of Leander's accident that left him lame is true, as is his statement that "If my leg goes, I'm going with it." Some readers may recognize Leander's nephew, Arthur Jordan. He did indeed fight in the Civil War. He died of his injuries after surviving a prisoner of war camp. His wife, Phebe Beach, was a good friend of Leander's. You can read more of their story in *Wild Sweeps the Wind.*

Civil War Echoes: Three of the characters—**Jane Small, Silas Andrews, and Marylou Hutchins**—all suffer losses due to the Civil War. In 1880, the country was only fifteen years past the devastation of that conflict. It cast a long shadow, leaving behind countless widows, orphans, wounded veterans, and the deep trauma of immense loss and bloodshed. Like many real veterans, the character Silas Andrews suffers from "soldier's heart," what we now recognize as Post-Traumatic Stress Disorder.

Senator Nat Libby: Senator Nat Libby is a fictional character. While he bears a slight resemblance to a prominent Bridgton figure with a similar name, no direct comparisons should be drawn between the two. The entire storyline involving Hannah Littlefield, the circumstances of Edwin's birth, the fire, and the subsequent subterfuge are all products of fiction.

Nan Sanborn: Nan Sanborn is fictional. While the 1880 Census lists a ten-year-old daughter named Addie living with the Sanborns at the Town Farm, she did marry and divorce, but not to Edwin, nor to the fictional Simon Libby. I used her as inspiration to create the character of Nan, providing Edwin with the love story I believe he deserved. I originally intended to name her Annie in the book, but after reconnecting with a member of the real Sanborn clan, I renamed her Nan to honor a family member.

The Pastors: Reverend Holland B. Frye and Reverend William Bailey Hague are real. Their personalities are as remembered by parishioners. Rev. Hague served two pastorates with the South Bridgton Congregational Church. Rev.

Frye served for a brief time. He did, indeed, disappoint the young people by forbidding the use of the church vestry for any but religious activities. And, yes, his picture was hung in the "indoor outhouse." (In later years, a "modern" bathroom was built in the same place. "Someone" (okay, it was me) hung Rev. Frye's photo back on the wall in the new bathroom.

The Attack on the Matron: The Matron of the Denmark Town Farm was, in fact, attacked as written. Her attacker, Arthur Blabon, was a real person who worked as a day laborer at various Town Farms in the area. This incident, combined with a separate attack by an Exeter man, likely created a pervasive sense of fear for families overseeing the running of Town Farms across the region.

The Pondicherry Town Farm: Based on the Bridgton Town Farm. The real Bridgton Town Farm closed in the 1940s, having outlived its usefulness and due to failing infrastructure. The house still stands today and is privately owned. The "old soldier feller" Edwin mentions, who put aside money for the "worthy and industrious" poor, was Lt. Robert Andrews. He fought at the Battle of Bunker Hill, and his grave marker in the South Bridgton Cemetery is easy to find. It's in the shape of the Bunker Hill monument.

Pondicherry Chronicles: Based on our hometown newspaper *The Bridgton News.* We are fortunate to have the extensive archives of the newspaper available in digitized form on the Bridgton Public Library website. Newspapers tell the stories of what people cared about, worried about, and got angry about in all the years they cover.

What's Next in the *Tales of Pondicherry* Series?

Town Farm Boy is just the beginning of a multi-book, multi-year project exploring the mythical town of Pondicherry and its fascinating inhabitants.

Next up is **Widow Foster's Ledger**, a tale of a woman navigating a man's world, running a woolen mill in Pondicherry in the absence of her husband. I wanted to write a book that combines my love of history with my career experience in business and accounting.

Beyond that, you can look forward to stories of four sisters coming of age amid tragedy, a patent medicine man, echoes of the Salem witch trials, and a poignant tale of a journey home. Or at least, that's what the voices in my head tell me. Join me!

Caroline D. Grimm